SWORD
BOOK SEVEN

Robert Ryan

Cover design by www.damonza.com

ISBN: 9798867758202
(print edition)

Trotting Fox Press

Contents

1. The Fields of Rah

Shar was at a crossroads. She had stepped so far forward in her rebellion that there was no going back. All that was left to her was to push forward. Yet in what direction?

Her armies were vast now, and the fate of the land rested on her shoulders. She could no longer make choices by herself. She must allow herself to be influenced by others, to be persuaded or dissuaded by their arguments, to allow those whom she ruled to have a part in the decisions that must come. And some were of enormous consequence.

Her western army had recovered from their battle. Victory had given them confidence. The decimation of some of their force had given them awareness of what could go wrong without proper care. It was a good combination. It was confidence tempered by caution.

From the north, a cold wind blew. It brought no snow, but it was deadly to those who were sick or had been injured. Many of the wounded who had survived the recent battles had died under its influence. The weather was as much an enemy to her as the shamans and the Nagrak hordes.

That was not quite true though. The weather could be her friend, too. It was a part of her current environment and situation, just as terrain, troop morale and equipment were in battle. All were tools at her disposal, and if she used them better than the enemy she would have the victory.

If the enemy were smarter than she, and used circumstances better, the victory would be theirs.

Pulling her hood up against the wind, she went in search of Radatan. He was not hard to find. As was often the case, he was playing dice with a band of soldiers.

The hunter turned tracker threw the bone dice, and laughed while his comrades muttered.

"Another win, Radatan?" she asked.

One of the soldiers grunted. "He always wins."

"He has luck," Shar agreed. "That's one of the reasons I like him."

Radatan grinned at her, and he looked just like Kubodin for a moment.

"I thought you liked me for my good looks?"

"That too. But mostly your good luck. Hopefully it doesn't run out over time as your looks have."

The soldiers chuckled. They liked this sort of byplay with their leaders. It made them seem approachable. Probably Radatan had set her up for the joke with that very purpose in mind. Just like Kubodin, he was far shrewder than he looked.

"You're a cruel general, Shar Fei. Just when I thought you were starting to like me, you knock me down."

"Well, if you keep winning at dice someone has to pull you back a bit. Otherwise you might get a big head."

"It's not as big as his money bag," one of the soldiers muttered.

"Then I'll spare you from him, at least for a little while. And who knows? I might even take his place for tomorrow's game."

Radatan stood and they walked a little to the side. The afternoon sun slanted in on them, and the little man squinted at her.

"What can I do for you, Nakatath?"

4

Just like that he was serious again, and she knew her earlier instinct had been correct.

"Any news yet from your scouts?"

"Not yet."

He gestured eastward. "The Fields of Rah are vast, and the enemy are on horseback. It'll take time to learn anything."

That was what worried her. She felt like a rabbit on the open grasslands, with eagles circling all around but so high up she could not see them.

"We're going to have to march without word of what's ahead. Speed is too important an asset to us."

Radatan scratched his head. "Well, if any of the enemy were close, the scouts would have returned sooner. So it should be safe enough, for a while. But march to where?"

That was the question, and again he showed his shrewdness. She had options. Plenty of them, but which one was the correct one to take?

"We need a war council," she said. "And swiftly. It's my fault. I should have realized the scouts would take longer than this. I had hoped for more information before making a choice, but time presses."

"Shall I gather the chiefs?"

"Yes. There's a large fire near my tent. We'll gather there."

The little hillman gave her a nod and walked away. She did note he gave a rueful glance at the group of soldiers still playing dice as he passed them. They, in turn, seemed just as glad he was going. The luck usually seemed to be his, and that was why she had him in mind for what must come next. If the generals agreed to it.

She went back to her tent, and drank some watered wine. Asana was there, waiting.

"What news?' he asked.

"Nothing yet. The scouts haven't returned."

"But you have a plan?"

"I do. Unless someone can suggest a better one. Everyone should be here shortly for a war council."

"Good," the swordmaster replied. "The men are enjoying a rest just now, but it'll be best to give them some direction soon. Idle hands breed trouble, and there are multiple tribes here that are only just getting used to each other."

It was not long before the chiefs began to arrive, and Shar came out of her tent and fed the fire herself. It blazed up, but they had to sit close to it for the warmth to penetrate.

She looked around. These were intelligent men, and some of them experienced. Boldgrim, Chun Wah and Asana most of all. But there were others such as Huigar whom she trusted, and whose counsels she heeded. It was not a requirement to be a chief to give advice in her war councils, only that the advice be well-considered and competent. In that, she knew she differed from the shamans. They followed a strict protocol based on seniority, but age was no surety for wisdom.

"We are at a crossroads, my friends," she began. "Kubodin holds Chatchek Fortress for us, and commands a large army. And here, we have a large army too. But what are we to do now?"

Asana gazed into the flames, his fingers fondling the hilt of his sword.

"We could strike for Nagrak City. That's the head of the serpent. Cut it off, and the enemy is dead."

"Do we have the numbers for that?" Shar asked.

The swordmaster looked uneasy. "I don't know. It's been a long time since I was in the city or wandered Nagrak lands. Their numbers are vast, but not limitless. Many must also be at Chatchek."

"If we attack Nagrak City, that might change," Radatan said. "If threatened, surely they'll send word for the soldiers at Chatchek to return."

Shar was not so confident. "Maybe. But if so, then Kubodin would be free to join us. That, the enemy would want to prevent at all cost. They might keep their troops at Chatchek to keep him penned up, and take their chances with us."

The chiefs thought about that. No one could be sure what would happen. In the end, it came down to how the enemy preferred to fight – all together in one front, or piecemeal. That, and whether or not they thought they could break through at Chatchek.

"I'm not sure they could keep their calm," Asana said. "If we marched toward the capital, with the force we have here, panic would set in. They'd scramble to bring all possible forces back to protect themselves. And the wealth they have accumulated in the city."

Shar inclined her head, but said nothing. What Asana argued was logical.

Maklar rubbed his hands together before the fire. "It's all well and good to talk of marching, but wherever you march the worst enemy of all remains. Winter. Men will die of cold."

There were nods of agreement to that.

"Do you propose establishing a camp here, ready to strike out as soon as the weather warms?" Shar asked.

"It would be safer," Maklar said.

"Perhaps. But men will die of cold even if we establish a camp."

There were nods of agreement to that too.

"Nor can we be sure the enemy won't march, even if we don't," Boldgrim said. "Of old, fighting in winter was no more popular than now, but it was done often enough. There are shamans who will remember that, and

7

who will know that it may offer them the advantage of surprise, even if it comes at a cost."

Radatan cleared his throat. "I'd do none of those things. I'd march straight to Chatchek. Kubodin needs our help, and if we combined forces with him, then we would have the largest army assembled in the Cheng Empire for a thousand years. Together, even the Nagrak hordes would fear us. Who could stop us then?"

There was much agreement to that, and the idea was discussed at length while the smoke from the fire curled around them in fits as the wind gusted.

Nogrod and Dastrin did not agree though. They argued, with persuasive force, that soldiers would die on the open plains. It might be better to wait, if necessary, to retreat into Nahlim Forest. There, if nothing else, there would be a little shelter and firewood aplenty.

"And what of food?" Shar asked.

There was no good answer to that. The army had supplies, but they would not last all winter. It was doubtful that the villages in the forest could provide enough. More could be brought from Skultic, but the enemy could cut off that line of supplies.

The conversation continued, but no real decision was made. Shar kept her thoughts to herself. It would be time soon enough to reveal what she had decided, or a part of it.

At any rate, their discussion had informed her course of action. What she chose to do would meet with approval, at least by many of them. It was the best she could hope for.

Asana sat in silence now, fingering the abbot's ring. She knew his thoughts were on revenge for Master Kaan. He had given his advice, but other than that he would follow where she led.

She did not doubt that Bai-Mai was around somewhere, plotting. He would show up at some point. Without the ring, he had no legitimacy as abbot himself. Even with it, few would follow him. But that was not how he thought. Either way, Asana was his enemy, and the fight that had been delayed must sooner or later come to pass.

2. Impenetrable as Midnight

The fire had begun to burn low by the time Shar spoke. The embers grew red, and the heat they gave was steady.

"You all make good points. This is how I see things though, and what I propose."

She rubbed her hands together. Despite the heat from the embers, the cold pierced her. She was used to a warmer climate and felt the cold more than many of those around her. Chun Wah seemed completely unaffected, but part of that might have been his training in the monastery.

"I will not retreat," Shar said. "What few soldiers we could save from the cold by heading into the forest, far, far more would die later when the Nagraks come against us. Only by force of speed and surprise can we hope to keep our casualties lower. Only by attacking the enemy when they are least prepared."

Radatan poked at the embers with a branch, and the tip blazed into light. Smoke swirled once more, and she felt the attention of her generals fixed on her. They had learned that she would do the unexpected, and they were waiting to see what that would be.

"What I propose is this. We'll strike toward Nagrak City. And fast. Let them fear us! It may even cause panic, as has been suggested. We are a large army now, and battle tested. We also have Boldgrim, to offer assistance against magic, for the closer we get to the city, the more the chance of shamans coming against us. They will be afraid of us, and so they should be."

Asana had stopped fingering his ring. Instead, his hand now fell to his sword hilt. Of late, he had lost a little of the calm that was such a hallmark of his personality. Yet by the way he gazed at her, she knew he was waiting for more.

"That is what they'll think. It may be enough for them to disengage at Chatchek. Whatever they do though, we will veer away and drive straight to Chatchek as fast as we may. If the siege is broken, we'll enter the fortress and overwinter there. If not, we'll break it and do the same."

That raised a few eyebrows, and the chiefs thought through it.

"A good plan," Dastrin said. "I like it."

Shar smiled. "As the old saying goes, let your plans be impenetrable as night, and strike like lightning from the dark."

The others all agreed, and their course of action was set. Only Asana remained silent, and he gazed at her off and on. No doubt, knowing her better than all the others, he had detected something. And well he might, but this was not the time to discuss it.

Arrangements were made, and the word was sent out to the soldiers. Tomorrow they would march, and Nagrak City was the direction they headed. As word spread, cheers went up in the camp, and a mood of excitement built.

The fire died down until even the embers darkened, and the generals went their separate ways. All had responsibilities, and organizing their men and talking to them in order to monitor morale was chief among them. But she signaled Boldgrim and Radatan to stay.

"What is it, mistress?" Radatan asked. Shar grinned at him. She liked the respectful informality of the term.

But she turned to Boldgrim first. "Can you talk to your brethren back in Chatchek?"

Shulu had told her that shamans could communicate by magic. She knew as much about them as they did themselves. *Know your enemy*, Shulu had often said.

Boldgrim pursed his lips in thought. "I can try. The distance is less than it was, and that helps. But it is not a magic I am good at."

"Then make the attempt. If you cannot, keep trying, for we will surely be getting closer day by day."

The shaman nodded. "And what shall I tell them?"

There was a look in Boldgrim's eyes that told her, despite her stated plan, that he was waiting for something more.

"Tell them all that has happened. Tell them to keep holding on. Tell them that help, one way or another, is coming."

Boldgrim narrowed his eyes. The answer had been a little vague, and they both knew it. Nevertheless, he bowed and departed for his own tent.

"And what can I do for you, Shar Fei?" Radatan asked.

"The greatest task of all," she replied.

The old hunter laughed at that. "You always have a trick up your sleeve. Some of the others suspect it. As well they should. I'm surprised you didn't tell Boldgrim though."

"He'll learn in due course."

"No doubt."

She looked at Radatan, and she did so with great fondness. He had been with her for what seemed a very long time now, but she was going to send him into great danger. She did not wish to, but there were few others in the world that she trusted as much, and he had the skill

12

for the task. And the luck. Both were things he would need.

The embers gave little warmth now, and the cold breeze blew through her. She shivered, but it was not only the cold that made her do so.

She hardened her heart. All the time she protected her friends, but sometimes she must send them into danger because they were the best person for what must be done.

3. Five Thousand Men

"I have a task for you, Radatan. What I told the others was ... let's call it misdirection rather than a lie."

He did not seem surprised. "You fear a spy in the camp?"

She gazed into the dying embers. "I do. How could there not be? There are many men in the army, and it only takes one to pass on word to the enemy. He could slip away in the night, and who would be any wiser? Probably there are several who are bought and paid for by the shamans. And others who might see an opportunity to gain favor or increased power."

"That's the nature of war," Radatan agreed. "Information is worth more than a thousand swords." He paused, and then grinned. "You can trust few people, but I'm glad you trust me."

Shar felt guilt creep up on her. It was not that she did not trust the others. It was that she must exercise extreme care. Her life hung in the balance, and likewise the future empire.

"Trust is a two-edged sword," she replied.

He slowly eased himself back on the cut log on which he sat.

"Well, now we come to it. What's my mission? A dangerous one, I think. No matter. I agree."

Shar felt warmth spread through her. She had chosen well, and his loyalty was humbling.

"I'll tell you. It *is* dangerous. Very dangerous. But I'll give you five thousand men. That's an army of your own

14

to command, and whatever the danger, it should, with luck, be enough to succeed."

Radatan squinted in thought. "That's too few to even think about going against Nagrak City. So what's the real target?"

"We need shelter from the cold," Shar replied. "I'll not go back into the forest, and little good that would do anyway. And we need food too."

"So what is it? There are villages aplenty on the Fields of Rah."

"So there are. But we need more than a village. I want a place that is large, and can be defended. And there is such a place, and fairly close. It gains its wealth from the fertile flood plains of the Ngar River a little to our east. They grow great quantities of grain, and store it there for distribution over all the Nagrak lands, and beyond."

"I see," Radatan said. "I've heard of the place. It's said the homes of the town are carved into a rocky cliff near the river. They have made it a natural fortress, secure against attack. Or at least difficult to overcome."

"Tashkar, it's called," Shar said. "It was built in my forefather's time, after he secured the empire against the shamans. Or so he thought. He feared they might try to stir rebellion against him by destroying the grain harvest and causing a famine. So he had their homes and massive granaries built into the stone of the cliffs."

"It won't be easy."

"Nothing ever is. Your mission is to take the town though, and gain possession of the grain before the enemy moves a force there to protect or transport it. Already they'll be planning one or the other. You must be swift, and if you succeed, you must hold it until the rest of our army gets there. Your force is a strike force. Rapid march. Push hard. Travel with few supplies so you can go faster. Use surprise to get there quicker than anyone would think possible. You leave at dawn."

Radatan stretched his legs. "I had best prepare then, and select my troops."

"There is more," Shar said.

"Speak on then, Nakatath. I've learned with you that there usually is."

"Crossing the Ngar river won't be easy. There must be some men, if not many, from Skultic or Nahlim that have traveled that way. Find them, and seek their assistance. I want you to find the best crossing for the army that will follow. It'll be slower and more cumbersome than yours, weighed down with more equipment and supplies."

Radatan frowned. "Finding a good crossing for a large army will slow me down. But if I find the right man who has been there before, it shouldn't be a problem."

"Find that man, Radatan. Find him and use his knowledge. Likely he knows the river valley too, and has been to Tashkar to trade."

When Radatan had gone, Shar sat by herself, deep in thought. She was sending him into great danger. His task was difficult, and if the enemy had moved faster than she, he was at risk of confronting a much larger force. Not only would he be killed, but she would lose five thousand warriors. She could ill afford either loss, but it was a risk worth taking. If she secured those grain supplies. She could feed her army, overwinter in a place of warmth, and deprive the enemy of vital supplies.

She had not told him her full plan though. And he had not asked. From Tashkar, she could still strike out toward either Nagrak City or Chatchek Fortress. Or she could wait the winter out. Better that no one knew what she intended. She had felt them all out though, and knew what they advised. In the end, she would adopt one of their plans. They need not know which one yet, and in truth she had not decided herself.

It would be time enough to decide what to do when she commanded in Tashkar. It was a choice she was happy to put off though. With the size of the armies now involved, any battle would spill the blood of thousands of warriors. It was a burden she could do without. Yet what other means was there but battle to throw off the yoke of the tyrannical shamans?

4. Smoke and Destruction

The sun was swiftly rising, red on the horizon, and Radatan and his five thousand men had already marched for an hour.

Squinting, and shading his eyes against the glare with a hand, he gazed out over the Fields of Rah.

"What a place to live," he said to Chun Wah. He had discovered the former monk had traveled for the monastery, buying supplies and healing the sick. It was their practice to wander the lands, and unlike ordinary warriors they were generally free to do so.

"I know. It's just so flat," Chun Wah replied.

It was not what Radatan meant. To him, the place was lifeless because there were no trees. Perhaps it was just a case of all the tribes loving their own lands where they were born and bred. It did not matter where it was. It was home, and they loved it.

There was no sign of anyone. Even Shar's army, which about now would be starting to march, was left behind as a smudge in the distance. He could barely see it. Perhaps, when they had traveled for a while the dust of their passage would rise and be more visible.

He signaled it was time for a rest. March for an hour, and rest for ten minutes. That was the old method they used in the Wahlum Hills, and he was going to stay true to it. He doubted his ancestors ever set the fast pace he did though. The flat land and lack of trees was good for something, at least.

"The Ngar River is close?" he asked Chun Wah as they shared water from a flask.

"Very. There are few trees along its banks, so it's hard to see from a distance. But we'll get there shortly."

"And the best crossing place? Not just for us but the rest of the army that follows?"

"There are several. Or there were. But the river changes a little each time it floods. And the ice is hard to predict. What suited a small band such as I traveled in might not be thick enough for an army."

That was true. Just as bad, the army would be vulnerable as they crossed. The enemy could use archers on them to great effect, or even attempt to fire the ice with brushwood. The sooner he got to the other side, safely, the better he would feel.

He called an end to the rest, and the men marched again. Shar had not misled him. This was a dangerous task, for to march at the speed he set was to leave the men tired. If they were attacked, they would be worn out before they even drew their weapons. There was also the risk of starvation. If they could not capture Tashkar, their supplies would run out quickly. Lightening their load was the only way they could march at the pace he set, and keep doing so for extended periods. He intended to carry on well into the night.

Shar would not be that far behind him. But if an enemy force separated them, he and his men were finished. Cold and hungry, they would succumb to death quickly without ever a blade being raised against them.

The morning passed without incident. Soon scouts returned. As yet, they had not located any enemies. That much was good. But the river took them longer to reach than he hoped. When they came to it, it was only half frozen.

"I suggest we go upstream," Chun Wah said. "The river is narrow here and flows more swiftly. There's a place to the south where it's wider, and the flow of water is less, so it may be properly frozen over."

That made sense, but it also took them away from Tashkar. Radatan did not like it. Time, as Shar demonstrated so frequently, was a weapon. And here he would lose some.

What could not be helped must be endured though, and Radatan gave the order to march upstream. The wind had calmed, but what slight breeze there was rustled eerily through the dried grasses.

The morning wore on. At times Radatan marked their path with overturned stones, or by piling a few together in various ways. It was hardly needed for the trampling of five thousand men was an easy track to follow. Yet Shar would have some of his scouts with her that would interpret his signs too. *No sign of enemy.* And *hastening forward.*

It was little enough. The sign he most wanted to leave was *crossed river and heading to target.* It would come in due course though.

He studied the country as he went. He did not like it. Flat and treeless, it seemed empty and void of life to him. He did note the flat and deep soiled plains on both sides of the river though. There were few rocks to use here as markers, and often he made notches on the trunks and branches of small bushes. Where he did find rocks, he noted how loose and loamy the soil was.

It was no surprise that grain was grown here. Though this side of the river was just grass, he could see the remnants of ancient fields and irrigation ditches. Neither were in use now, and had not been for a very long time. Perhaps nothing had been cultivated here since the assassination of Chen Fei and the disintegration of the empire.

From what he could see of the east bank, it was different there.

They moved ahead at great pace, but warily. The scouts did not go far afield. Rather, they stayed close and kept watch for an ambush. Though there was little enough in the way of terrain to conceal any number of troops, at times deep gulleys ran through the loamy soil toward the river. Companies of horsemen could hide in such places, and the speed of their mounts made them dangerous if they attacked while the approaching army was unaware of them.

The scouts found no ambushes though. After a few more swift marches, and short rests, the scouts delivered news of a crossing ahead. It was wide, but the ice seemed strong. Proof of this was that a large group of riders had recently passed over. Yet there was no sign of them on the other side. They appeared to have headed off toward Nagrak City.

Radatan did not trust appearances. He did trust his scouts though. The way ahead was clear, and they crossed at noon. Lunch would have to wait until they got to the other side. Only then, with the scouts spread out around them in a protective half circle, would he feel safe enough to call a longer rest.

The crossing was slow and difficult. Despite the riders moving over the ice, it was hardly what he would call safe. The ice was not of an even thickness, and it occurred to him that the Nagraks, who would know this crossing better, had chosen a narrow path whereas he and his five thousand men must move over a much wider surface. It could be a kind of trap, intended to mislead them.

Despite his fears, they came safely to the other side. Here the bank drew up steeply, and then topping it the ground was perfectly flat. He gave the order for the men to eat a cold lunch. He was not going to signal his presence to the enemy by smoke, if he could help it.

He and Chun Wah sat together eating in silence. All they had was some dried meat, and a little stale bread. The same as what all the men had. And water from the frozen river, crushed down and only half melted to drink.

They did not talk much. Both were quiet men, and Radatan liked it that way. When Chun Wah spoke though it was usually to a good purpose. They were very different in many ways, and their homes, tribes and experiences could not be further apart. Yet Radatan felt a kinship to him. At heart, both were warriors who preferred the simple pursuits of hunting and farming.

The other grew still, then stood, his gaze fixed as though on something far away to the north-east.

Radatan grew wary. "What is it?"

"Smoke."

That was all the former monk said, but it was enough. Radatan stood too, and followed the direction the other man was looking.

It was a long way away. Or perhaps the fire that caused it had only just started. The smoke was a thin plume, bent sideways quickly as the breeze took it.

"It was not there moments ago," Chun Wah said.

Radatan believed him. For the plume of smoke grew thicker as they watched, and it became clearer that it was closer than it had at first appeared.

"Is there a village that way?" Radatan asked.

"There are several in that direction. Most are close to each other here for the fertile land is only a narrow band by the river. But there's more smoke than you usually see from a village."

Radatan agreed, but he said nothing. There was no point in guessing. Anyway, they would find out soon enough. To the north-east was the path they must take themselves, and they would come close to the smoke.

He gave word for the march to begin again. There was some grumbling from the men. They were covering a great deal of ground in a short space of time, but he had learned from observing Shar.

Truly, anything was possible under Shar Fei's leadership. She did the unexpected. She outwitted her enemies. She insulted and infuriated them, all with a cool mind to maneuver an advantage. And so often she did. She had the fierce heart of a hill cat, the wisdom of a timber wolf and the clear sightedness of an eagle. When the time came, she would make the perfect emperor.

If it came. It was his task now to help take her one step closer to that, and there was nothing he would not do to fulfill his mission. He was nothing but a hill man. Nothing but a hunter with tracking skills, and some experience of battle. But she had seen something in him, and given him great responsibility.

He was not a noble. Or connected by some machination. It was not about favors, or bribes or schemes as it always was among the shamans. She selected him because she thought he was best for the task, and an empire that worked on that principal instead of shadowy strings of influence was an empire that could rise to rule the world.

If it wanted to. Shar was not that sort of leader. Yet who could say how she would think once she had defeated the shamans and ruled with supreme authority for years? Might not such ultimate power change her? It was said Chen Fei had changed in his later years. But many things were said about him. Much of it the whisperings of shamans who tried to poison the minds of the people.

23

For the most part, they had not succeeded. After years, it might even have turned against the shamans like a knife mishandled that cut the wielder. For the more the shamans said how bad Chen Fei was, the more the people yearned for the return of someone like him to rule. Someone who fought for all the people and united them rather than divided.

They marched over some empty fields. They were not in use now, but on this side of the river it was clear they had seen recent use. Perhaps not for a few years, but recent by comparison to the other side.

So too were the field divisions more clearly demarked. In places this was done by building a low wall of stones. But as there seemed to be few stones in the deep soil, and they most likely were carried in from further away where the land rose gently, this was far less common than borders of short hedges.

The stone walls were no obstacle to the army. The men easily crossed them. The hedges, in places, grew wild and thick. They were harder to get through. And they presented a danger of ambush.

Radatan deployed all his scouts, but he kept them close to the army. An ambush could hardly go undetected. Even so, he skirted wide of the thicker hedges. And ever he kept a sharp eye on the rising smoke. Whatever the cause was, it boded ill.

"I can smell the smoke," Chun Wah said. The monk marched with a hand hovering at times close to his sword hilt. He felt the same unease Radatan did.

There was nothing to do but move ahead. Scouts returned at times and reported, and they brought news of a large village ahead. There were buildings on fire, but the scouts had not yet entered.

Radatan understood that. It smelled of a trap. Still, the enemy had not been seen, at least yet, and his own army was now making good time.

The fields changed. Here, they had been planted to grain and harvested. Stubble remained, and the earth had not yet been ploughed for a new crop, nor would be until spring now. The earth was hard and cold, and even patched by a remnant of snowfall in places.

By chance, or design if the enemy guessed Radatan's destination, the village was close to their chosen path. He veered a little toward it. Better to face any attack head on than be caught trying to skirt it.

The scouts now reported no sign of anyone there though, but they also said because of fire and smoke they could not search adequately.

By the time they reached it the fires had died down somewhat, but the smoke still hung heavy and acrid in the cold air. Radatan took a column of a hundred men, Chun Wah with him, to sweep the village and confirm there was no ambush.

They entered upwind of the smoke, and trod warily in tight formation, down the main track. There was no sign of people at all, nor any signs of an attempt to put out the destructive flames. It seemed strange, but Radatan was beginning to understand.

Moving ahead, they took side paths now and then. A hut collapsed to their left, and the flames roared to life as new thatching and timber was exposed to hungry tongues of fire. The heat was intense, and they passed on quickly.

The village was empty. Devoid of people, and devoid of livestock. There was only the burning houses.

Radatan gritted his teeth. "You know what this is?" he said to Chun Wah.

The monk nodded. "It is the enemy themselves. They are scourging the country before we arrive. They leave no places for us to shelter, nor any food to sustain ourselves."

He was right, and Radatan felt fury build up inside him. No chief would order this. At least he did not think so. It was shamans' doing, and they cared nothing of the lives and work they destroyed. Radatan would have left the village alone so long as no contingent of soldiers was stationed there.

The column left the desolate village, but Radatan knew it would be a long time before the smell of smoke, destruction and callousness left him. It was a sign of what to expect though. The enemy were harsh, and they gave no quarter, even to their own.

They rejoined the rest of the army and pressed ahead. Radatan pushed even harder now. The Nagraks might have guessed Shar's plan. Or maybe they were just destroying any possible source of food over a large swathe of country all around. Either way, he could not be sure. But if they fortified Tashkar with extra troops before he reached it, he might fail Shar.

He hardened his heart and stepped even that little bit quicker at the head of the army. What he could do, they could do. They *must* do it, even if they came to a battle situation tired and worn out. He would not let Shar down, and speed was his ally. As she had proved so often, it saved lives in the end.

They had not gone far though when scouts started to return. They warned of mounted men ahead.

Radatan did not slow. He kept going, and he marched directly toward Tashkar. If there was a force in his way, he would destroy it.

If he could. But if it outnumbered him, then all was lost. Shar would not thank him for getting five thousand of her men killed needlessly, but his mission would have failed. What would she do then?

He hoped not to find out. Reports of the size of the force ahead were vague though. Yet soon he saw for himself. Even as he marched at them, they rode toward him.

The enemy were still too far away to see properly, or to judge their numbers. Likely, they were the same warriors who fired the village. Radatan almost wanted a confrontation with them, but any delay meant more time for other troops to reach Tashkar.

5. Riders on the Plain

The sun slipped from its high point in the sky, and began its quick descent toward the horizon and dusk. The wind had picked up again, and it blew colder. It whispered through the dry seed heads of the sere grass, and rattled the stubble and threshed remains of the last crop in those places where the army traversed a field recently in use.

Inexorably, the two forces grew closer quickly. Radatan marched with haste. The Nagraks trotted on ponies. Neither veered away, sought better ground, or waited.

There was no better ground. Not on open plains such as this. The scouts reported the two armies to be of similar size.

Radatan was not so sure that mattered. The Nagraks were mounted. That gave them a longer reach, and if the horses were tired the men who rode them were less so. Yet Shar's tactics had been proven against such an aggressor.

If infantry held its ground, and erected a wall of spears before it, the horses would not trample the soldiers. They were strong against such an attack, and could kill the riders whereas the riders struggled to reach them with swords before dying.

It was the critical concept. Would the men hold their position, or turn their backs and flee at the approach of a thundering charge? It was not easy to summon the courage to stand firm before that, but the men had seen it done, and seen the tactic victorious.

Radatan sent a message to all his men to remind them. *If battle comes, hold your ground. The enemy will crash against us and die. Turn your backs, and it will be you.*

The enemy host came close enough now that they could be clearly seen. They rolled forward in an easy trot, giving no sign that they would stop.

Radatan consulted Chun Wah. "What do you think?"

"They'll try to scare us first. To see if their charge causes us to panic and retreat. Or worse, to scatter."

That seemed likely true. Radatan thought for a moment, and then he gave orders. He would send his army straight at the enemy. Not veering aside, nor even coming to a standstill. Most of all, not retreating. They held a good formation, and they were men of courage who had recently fought and won. He had confidence in them.

The Nagraks came on in a mighty rush. The sound of the horse hooves grew loud, and then thunderous. On top of that, the Nagraks screamed and yelled, creating as much noise as they could.

Radatan smiled grimly. "You were right. They're trying to scare us. But look at their numbers. They're no more than us, and I don't think they'll finish the charge off. Unless we break ranks, many of them will die."

Chun Wah strode ahead, sword in hand. He did not take his eyes from the enemy.

"You might be right. It depends how stupid their leader is. If so, he will go through with it. If not, he will veer aside. They must have had word of the previous battles. They know what will happen if they cannot get us to break formation."

There was nothing to do but march forward. Spearmen had come to the front ranks, and Radatan and Chun Wah were close behind. They did not wield spears, but they would be close to give direction to the fight and take part if the front rank collapsed.

The enemy drew within fifty paces, and showed no sign of stopping. Radatan, for his part, was going to go through them, or die trying. Nothing was going to stop him from getting to Tashkar for Shar.

Except death.

The riders came on. The noise was deafening, but Radatan shouted over and above it in a cry that would have echoed for leagues in the canyons of the Wahlum Hills.

"Hold firm! Spears up! Watch them turn away like cowards!"

The riders came on. Radatan had been wrong. He knew it as they hurtled forward like a crashing storm to destroy. Yet at the very last instant, later than he would have thought possible, they veered to the side and raced away in sudden silence except for the hooves of the ponies that tore at the part-frozen earth, sending clods flying in their wake.

Radatan felt a moment of relief, and indecisiveness. But he knew he must act to take advantage of what had happened.

"Nagrak cowards!" he cried out.

"Pony-born misfits!" Chun Wah cried alongside him.

They were both trying to relieve tension and denigrate the enemy. The enemy that was laughed at was the enemy not feared.

He knew Shar, Kubodin or Asana would have acted more quickly than he had. He was learning from them though, and he would get better.

The soldiers had stood still in the last moment of the rush, and now some of them took up the calls. Many of them laughed, even if it was nervously. But they had held their ground for that first charge, the worst of all. If more came, Radatan did not think they could be moved. They would be solid as a fortress wall, and the enemy must realize that too.

"Forward!" Radatan commanded, and the army moved ahead. He was going to take the initiative, and see what the enemy did. It would reveal much about the leader's ability and intentions.

The Nagraks wheeled around in a great circle, and then came to a standstill far ahead, but still directly in the way of Radatan's path.

"What now?" he asked Chun Wah.

The other man shook his head doubtfully. "They may try us again, but to what purpose? We're even more likely to hold now that we have done it once."

Radatan agreed. He thought he knew what the Nagrak commander would do, and it would reveal what he wanted to know.

The men marched forward, and tired as they were they began to sing as they stepped. In their minds they had already beaten their opponent, and they could be forgiven for thinking so. It gave them confidence, but one victorious battle did not necessarily win the war.

Radatan had to look much further ahead than just what was playing out now, but then a slow smile spread over his face.

"There's your answer," Chun Wah said quietly.

Out of the Nagrak army some dozen riders began to trot forward. One was in the lead on a piebald pony that stepped proudly. He would be the commander. Behind him a man waved a cloth as a signal to parley. The others rode close behind, looking a little nervous as well they should.

"They seek a parley," Radatan said. "But only to delay our advance."

31

"You think we're still a chance of taking Tashkar then?"

"Of course. Why else try to delay us? If they could fight us here and win, they would. If they had a bigger army at Tashkar, they would merely retreat to it and wait for us."

"Maybe," the former monk said.

Radatan thought he was right. There was no way to be sure of anything though. He could only make the best choices that the information and circumstances he faced allowed. After that, it was up to the gods.

It was said in the Wahlum Hills that gods made the destinies of men. It was also said that men chose their gods. He did not believe much in either, but since traveling with Shar many strange things had happened.

Shar Fei. Nakatath. Who would have believed such a thing possible after all this time? The old emperor had been assassinated a thousand years ago, and yet still his line endured. And still Shulu Gan lived.

He felt a sense of awe gather around him. He lived in remarkable times, and Shar Fei had given him remarkable responsibility. He would not let her down, even if he had to fight through the army ahead by himself.

The enemy leadership group approached. The commander looked stern and proud. It was a look that Radatan, used to chiefs such as Kubodin, frowned upon. Those who held themselves up with arrogance were often the first to fall when blades were drawn. Or to run.

That was not the right way to think though. The enemy were Nagraks, and who knew how it was with them. They could not be measured by the standards of the Two Ravens Clan, and it would be dangerous to underestimate them.

No real attack had yet been made. It was clear they did not wish to, and that they sought to delay things. That did not mean though that they would not attack if forced into it, or that help was not near at hand for them. They might be delaying for that rather than to stop Shar's men reaching Tashkar. For surely by now they had deduced the destination of the five thousand men that marched over their land.

What should he do?

6. Onward

Radatan knew what must be done. It was against convention, but everything in this time of Shar Fei was.

It was no great breach of etiquette though. He would allow the enemy to disengage, should they choose.

The riders of the enemy force came on. Radatan signaled his army to keep marching, but now at a faster pace. He headed straight at the enemy.

Upon his piebald horse the leader gave no indication he was surprised, or upset, or even that he noticed the marching men at all. He could merely have been out on a ride to inspect the fields. The one near him with the flag of parley waved it wildly as Shar's army marched straight at him.

"Do you not heed the rules of law, man?"

It was their leader who spoke, and despite his appearance he could not hide the edge of surprise in his voice. Or maybe uncertainty. Whatever it was, Radatan enjoyed it.

"You're in the way, *man*. We're going straight ahead, whether you're there or not. It's no breach of parley. You'll be unharmed if you draw no weapon. But if your cavalry stays in our way we'll crush it beneath our boots."

The men behind Radatan gave a cheer as they marched, and the riders looked decidedly nervous now.

"We demand parley!"

"Make your demands while we march, if you like. I know you're trying to delay me. And it won't work. Nakatath has given me orders, and her decree will be fulfilled. So stay put little man, or ride away, or attack, I care not. Whatever you do, you're in our way."

The piebald grew agitated and stepped to the side before the rider reined it in sharply. He gave Radatan a cold look, haughty and full of dislike, then nudged his mount to turn and rode back to his army without saying anything further.

"You made an enemy of him," Chun Wah said.

"Good! The more he dislikes me the more hasty he'll be."

"He might attack."

"If he allows himself to be influenced so easily, he's an idiot."

Chun Wah laughed. "You sound just like Shar."

"I've been with her for what seems a long time now. She's rubbed off on me. She's far better than I am at getting under the skin of the enemy though."

They marched ahead, and the cavalry trotted away in an arc. Some of the men thought they were fleeing, but Chun Wah did not.

"You annoyed him, all right. He's going to attack."

Radatan thought so too. Perhaps he had brought this on, but in truth it was no bad thing. He believed now the men would withstand the assault. He had confidence in that, and it would only lower the morale of the enemy.

It might not be as it was last time though. There was no purpose in feinting again to try to get the infantry to break formation. This time they would engage.

They should get the worst of that. Spears would kill many Nagraks before the riders got close enough to use their curved sabers. Any battle was a risk though. He could not be sure how it would turn out.

He gave the order to stand still, and prepare for battle. Even as he did so the Nagraks gathered pace, and they turned at the end of the arc and charged straight at the infantry. They yelled and screamed as before.

"They'll engage this time!" Radatan cried out. "Hold firm!"

The riders hurtled down like a tempest of wind, thunder and fury. They did not stop, but turned at the last moment to rake sideways across Radatan's front line, swords flashing.

It was a more effective tactic than the previous one. Many riders died, or were thrown off their mounts as the spears thrust into the armor that some wore, or wounded their flesh rather than killed them outright. Even so, many other managed to get in close enough to slash with their swords.

The Nagraks, when they were close enough, targeted the arms of the spearmen as the easiest to reach part of their body. Such blows did not kill, but the men injured that way would not hold a spear again in this battle. If ever.

Many of the Nagrak who had fallen were trampled under the hooves of the seething mass of horses that jostled together in such a tight space. Others lived, and injured, rose as their brothers finished their raking movement and rode away.

Those men were unfortunate. The swordmen behind the front line raced through the gaps and slew them where they struggled to rise, and even chased after others who had begun to run. Few escaped that, but Radatan called them back. If they went too far the cavalry would make easy prey of them.

"Catch the ponies!" Radatan called out. At first the men ignored him, intent on ensuring the Nagraks laying sprawled on the grass really were dead. Then they tried for riderless ponies that stood nearby.

"Good thinking," Chun Wah said. "We may not get many, but each one will be valuable, especially for scouts."

"We won't need many," Radatan replied. "Few in our army know how to ride. But there'll be some."

"Hurry!" he called out again, directing his words at those men who tried to catch the ponies. The horses were spooked though, and many raced away.

The front rank reformed. Radatan snatched up a spear that had fallen from the hands of a dead comrade, and joined them. It was not his place as commander to fight, yet he had seen both Shar and Kubodin do it.

He knew why too. They gave heart to those they commanded that way. A leader was no leader unless he endured what his followers endured. Without that, respect diminished.

There was a time and a place for this too. A leader could not do it all the time. When the enemy made a great attack though, that was the opportunity to stiffen the resolve of those who defended against it. Such an attack was coming now.

The Nagraks could not afford more than one more try. Each time they attacked, they lost too many men. If they did not succeed now, they would shift to a different tactic. That meant though that they would give this everything they had.

"Here they come again!" he called out. "Stand strong and hold your ground, and you'll see the backs of the cowards one more time. Then we'll be off to Tashkar again. Nothing will stop us!"

The cavalry charged at them as before. It was different for Radatan now. He saw those riders coming clearly, galloping like a wave of terror about to crash over him. He felt fear rise up from his guts, and his hands shake. He felt the fright of the warriors close to him as they braced for the onslaught.

His respect for the men suddenly grew. They had faced this before and not broken. He would follow their example.

The mad rush hit them. It seemed far harder to Radatan this time than before, but maybe that was because he was now in the front line.

He held his ground. A roan pony nearly crashed into him, then turned abruptly. The rider leaned from the saddle, wicked sword gleaming and about to cut. He was lifted from his saddle by the force of a spear thrust into his abdomen by the man in the line next to Radatan.

Toppling, the rider screamed. That scream was cut short by hooves that trampled him.

The rest of the riders came on. Radatan got the knack of using his spear. Several times he wounded an attacker, but they turned and rode off before he could kill. Yet now his spear took a Nagrak warrior squarely, penetrating his leather jerkin and sliding through his abdomen.

As the rider fell, the spear was nearly ripped from Radatan's grip. He was pulled forward, nearly colliding with the pony that kicked at him as it sped away. Only by leaning to the side and the luck of the gods did he avoid being hit in the head.

The rider was still alive. Radatan pulled the spear free, and the man screamed. Another rider hurtled toward him, leaning forward in the saddle and aiming to decapitate him. The blade fell. The rider's horse leaped over the dying man and Radatan's spear came up, the tip tearing at the upper arm of his attacker.

At the last moment the leap of the horse unbalanced the rider, just as the spear struck him. It was not a killing blow, but he came from the saddle and landed heavily.

More riders came. Somehow the attacker scrambled out of their way and was lost in the churn of dust on the other side of them. Radatan stepped back into the line.

The point of the spear was red, and the tassel of cloth just below it, already red, dripped with gore. Yet, for the most part, it stopped blood running down the length of the shaft which would have made it too slippery to hold properly.

Radatan braced himself, getting a feel for this type of fighting now. It was not what he was used to, but the killing of men in battle was the same the world over. Only the tactics changed.

Once more the enemy came. Radatan glimpsed their leader on his piebald, aloof from his warriors and holding back to direct the next charge from the rear. He looked proud and confident, but it was an act. He was losing this battle, and both armies knew it.

That made the man dangerous. He must answer to shamans in the end, and he would not want to do that. Not after a loss. So he would throw all he had into the fray now, and instill, if he could, the fear of the shamans into his men.

The enemy reformed and charged again. They were less noisy this time. Only the ponies made a sound as they rushed forward, like a river roaring in flood. The men had learned to save their breath and conserve their energy. No tactic would frighten now. Only steel might work, and the courage of beating hearts that pumped blood to the arms that carried swords.

The forces crashed together. Still the horses shied away from the wall of spears, but the Nagraks, experts at controlling them, found what gaps they could in the defenses and edged into them in order to try to widen them.

This time groups of Nagraks dismounted too. They were not used to fighting on foot, but their normal tactics had failed. Yet Nagraks or not, they were still Cheng, and the very name of their race meant warrior.

The fighting was fierce. In those places where they got through the defenses their comrades, still mounted, tried to follow. But the defenders fought with great energy. Now the second line of defense was in play. Swordsmen.

Chun Wah was among them. He fought with a skill that Radatan could scarcely believe. The legend of the fighting monks was true, even if the man was no longer of that order.

The two of them now fought side by side. Radatan cast his spear into the approaching enemy, and now used his sword which he much preferred. Where the enemy started to break through, those two were there. At least as far as they were able to move up and down the line.

It was a fierce battle. The enemy were driven on by their leader who feared to report failure. The defenders fought for their lives in enemy territory, and to complete the task Shar Fei had set them. For her, they were willing to die.

So was Radatan. Even more than they, for he knew her better. Even so, he had no intention of doing that if it could be helped.

The Nagraks, driven as they were, remained a cavalry force at heart. They had no taste for fighting on foot, and soon their assault began to lose force.

Radatan read the mood. His own men sensed victory, and the enemy were disheartened.

"Slow march!" he ordered, and an aide close by blew his horn to signal the instruction to all.

Shar's army began to move. It was a step here and a step there at first. The Nagraks tried to resist, but like a mudslide in the Wahlum Hills that started slow and gathered unstoppable momentum, so did this.

The infantry pressed forward. The Nagraks gave way. Whether by order or by mutual fear, Radatan could not tell which, the enemy suddenly fled. Those on foot retreated to mounts held for them. Those on mounts wheeled and galloped away.

Radatan could not see the leader anywhere. A pity. He wished to see his face. He would not look so arrogant now.

Chun Wah wiped his bloody sword clean on the tunic of a fallen enemy before sheathing it.

"Now what?"

7. He Never Broke His Word

Radatan assessed the situation quickly.

The enemy must now know his destination. They had tried to delay him reaching it, even starting a battle they must have known they had no advantage in. That meant they were desperate to stop him.

His course of action was therefore clear. He must do precisely what the enemy did not wish.

"Gather what wounded we have," he ordered. "Set them on the captured ponies. Tie them if necessary. We march, and we march swiftly. Tashkar awaits us."

He knew the men were tired. They had marched long and fast, and now fought a battle. They did not like it, but he knew in the end it might spare them great grief. If only he could capture Tashkar, by one means or another, he would be secure until Shar, moving more slowly, could arrive with the bulk of the army.

Speed would help with that task. Delay might destroy all chance of success. If he did not take it, and got caught on the Fields of Rah where masses of the enemy might bear down on him without the protection of walls, he and his men would be ground to dust. A little pain now might save catastrophe later.

"Will we not even bury our dead?" one of the soldiers nearby asked.

"They died a warrior's death. I'll not let it be in vain. Better they go unburied than they died for nothing."

Soon after the army marched again. Radatan was at the front, setting the pace. He marched quickly, but not quite so quickly as before. He did not know how soon their next battle might be.

The Nagrak cavalry kept their distance. They were still there though, monitoring all developments. And no doubt sending word to other forces. Where were they? How close were they? What were their numbers?

He did not know.

The day wore on. The sun fell over the horizon of the world to its rest, but the army kept marching even as night enveloped all. They had been marching, it seemed, forever. When the tread of their boots did not weary them, the swinging of sword and thrusting of spear did. All about them were enemies, for they were in an enemy land. The dark might hide an ambuscade. It might hide the death they had so far evaded.

But the men marched, for Radatan marched before them. If he could endure, so would they. So too they knew that camping would only bring them greater danger. The enemy might attack at night. Attacking during the day had failed, so they would try something else. Or they may receive reinforcements. Whatever the case, it was best to do that which was least expected, and that meant marching beneath the stars even when bone-tired.

Radatan could see little of the land they passed. He could tell though, even in the dark, that more and more of it was cultivated. Many were the flat fields they traversed, wheat stubble rustling beneath their boots.

At times they heard the murmur and gurgle of the icy Ngar River to their left. Radatan kept close to the bank deliberately. Firstly, that ensured he would not get lost in the dark. Secondly, they should be secure from enemy attack from that direction.

The scouts extended ahead and behind, but mostly to the right. It was from there that an attack was likely to come should any be made. Yet the scouts found no one out there, and he began to think that he had lost the Nagraks in the dark. If so, it would not last long. They knew where he went, and come daylight they would find him again.

An advantage was an advantage though, and time was precious. Even a few hours might make all the difference in the world.

The night was old before they camped at last. Radatan was exhausted, and his left knee ached from walking. There was no slackening of effort though. A patrol was established. A perimeter guard was picketed, and the scouts spread farther afield.

They lit no fires for fear of undoing their hard work and revealing themselves. That meant no hot food. Radatan was on dangerous ground, for an ill-fed army fought badly. So too a tired one. But the men did not mind too much. They had won a victory today, and they could still eat well, even if it was not hot. Most of all, they could swiftly wrap themselves in cloaks and blankets and sleep.

Radatan did not. For hours he stayed awake, and the scouts returned to him regularly. The Nagrak riders were some way behind them, and they camped.

It was good news. Their own scouts must have reported they could not find the enemy, but they would not have expected them to march so far during the night. They would have a lot of catching up to do in the morning.

The army camped in the middle of a field. It had been ploughed after the previous harvest, and no doubt would be planted to a crop again as soon as spring came. That was not far away. Midwinter was on the land now, and through the night a scattering of sleet fell. It was the worst time of year to be marching, but if they could take

Tashkar, Shar would see out the worst of it in shelter and still be close to whatever target she chose to attack when the weather began to warm.

At last, he drifted to sleep. It seemed as though he had barely blinked though before a horn blew to signal the coming dawn, and to prepare for another day.

The march began in a roiling fog. It drifted up from the river and swathed the flat lands near it in a blanket of gray. It was fortunate, for it would help them deceive the enemy a little longer. It was even possible the enemy, thinking him close at hand, would not risk riding through the murk in case of an ambush. If so, his army might gain another few hours' march over and above what they had stolen by the great march last night.

Maybe. Radatan peered ahead into the seething gray air. It would not do to underestimate the enemy. They may or may not have been deceived, either by the forced march or this morning's weather. The leader might have split his force and sent riders ahead from the main camp the scouts had discovered.

So it might be that Radatan's men walked into an ambush. Nevertheless, he set a good pace and trusted to his scouts ahead to give warning.

The men were nervous. He sensed it all around him. They did not like the fog. In their own country they would think nothing of it. But here, in the land of the Nagraks, it could be hiding whole armies.

Who was to say it was not? Radatan felt his own unease grow. Logic kept his fears in check though. If there were other forces close by, the enemy commander would not have attacked yesterday. Instead, he would have joined with it, and with their greater force obliterated his own. If there was only a part of the force here they had encountered yesterday, they could easily defeat it.

45

The men marched, and they did so in silence. There was no singing. There was no joking. Even the tread of their boots was muffled by the heavy air all around them.

An hour they marched, and rested. A second hour they marched, and rested again. The fog remained unchanged, and a superstitious fear settled into the hearts of the warriors.

This was shaman's work, some muttered. Radatan did not think so though. Then suddenly the fog thinned. They came up a slight rise, and a bend in the river took them slightly to the east. The sun shot golden beams over the fields, and the stubble of the last crop flared golden.

They marched on. The fog dissipated entirely from around them, retreating to a band on their left that followed the river.

"There it is," Chun Wah said.

Radatan studied what lay ahead. It was a strange sight. It was Tashkar, and he had heard it described to him. The real thing was more strange than all the stories though. It was unlike any other Cheng city he had heard tell of.

The river had changed course in eons past. Although some said it was the engineers of Chen Fei who had diverted it deliberately. First, so as to better irrigate the fields, through which many hand dug irrigation channels ran, and second to make the city a fortress.

And fortress it was. It stood upon a buttress of hard rock that swelled hundreds of feet upward. To the left the river ran, or would do if it were not frozen. Although here, frozen it might be, but because the banks were narrow it ran more swiftly and the ice was thin and patchy. Even in midwinter no army could cross there.

To the right the course the river once ran was now dry, but uncounted seasons it had run there before and gouged out a deep declivity around the hard stone on which the city stood. That declivity ran along the front of the fortress too, making attack from the rear, right and the front extremely difficult.

Many men would die trying to take it. He had a large army though, and the element of surprise. If he could take advantage of it.

Surprise, if he had it, would not last long. On this he was soon surprised himself, however. Scouts began to return from the surrounds of the town, and they brought good news.

"They are fleeing, sir," one of them informed him.

"All of them?"

"It's hard to tell. It seems like women and children for the most part. So far, at least."

Radatan thought on that. The news was less good than he thought, and as more scouts came in they reported the same. Only women and children had left. Even that flow had now stopped.

He glanced at Chun Wah. "What do you make of it?"

"They don't flee in panic. It's a matter of mouths to feed. If there's a siege, now they can last longer."

Radatan had thought that too. "And yet what of their harvests and the stores of their grain? Should they not have enough food there to feed an army for years?"

The former monk grinned. "I've done business with these people. They're wealthy, and the wealthy are tighter with money than a noose around a steer's neck on the way to market. They have plenty of grain, but the more they eat themselves the less they have to sell and profit from."

That could well be true. Radatan hoped it was. It opened up a new way of attaining his mission. Shar had instructed him to take control of the city, and to fortify it for her later arrival. She had left it to him how to do that.

47

Battle was one way. So was intimidation. Bribery another, and it seemed the last might be the best way to achieve his goal. Assuming, at any rate, that avarice played as much a role in their character as Chun Wah suggested.

Shar had gold. Wherever she defeated shamans, she found it. In plenty. She would pay for all the grain she needed, and do so at a better price than these farmers would otherwise receive. That might be a means to victory without spilling a single drop of blood. And if it went poorly for Shar's army afterward, the people of the town could always tell the shamans they were forced into the arrangement.

Radatan struck forward at a fast pace. Scouts were everywhere, but still he kept looking around for signs of the Nagrak force from yesterday. He saw nothing.

It was a stroke of luck. No, it was his decision to force a march and the hard work of the army to implement it. Had they gone at a normal pace they might well be engaged in another battle now. Or more likely the cavalry would be merely skirmishing with them, and trying to slow them down.

He had avoided that. He had reached his destination, but now the hardest part of all was upon him. He did not have the numbers to lay siege to Tashkar and at the same time fight off the cavalry. Even if he did, how long before Nagrak reinforcements arrived?

Without doubt, word of yesterday's events, and his progress toward Tashkar, were already on their way back to Nagrak City. Reinforcements would certainly soon be coming, if they were not already on the way. Whatever he could do, he must do it fast.

At least the first half of his mission was fulfilled. He had prevented the enemy, so far as he could tell, from reinforcing Tashkar. They had tried to beat him yesterday in battle, and that had been a mistake. They should have left him alone and come here. Maybe they thought they could win. Maybe, being Nagraks, they had no desire to defend a city but preferred to fight on horseback. Whatever the case, it had been an error of judgement and the shamans would deal harshly with the leader.

Radatan put those thoughts from his mind. They approached close to Tashkar now, and all his attention must be on that.

Coming near, they saw a trail lead down deep into the dry river bank. It was narrow, being wide enough to allow only one wagon at a time through. That gave the inhabitants a way to transport their wealth of grain in and out of the city, but an attacking force only a narrow path.

To each side of the trail was a mess of sand, rocks, unstable banks and boulders that looked set to topple and slide the moment a foot was set anywhere near them.

"Not an easy place to attack," Chun Wah said with understatement.

"Let's see what diplomacy can do," Radatan replied.

A moment later he saw what he was hoping for. A delegation came out from the town. With a boom a great portcullis was lowered, and out of a cave, now revealed behind it, rode some half a dozen men.

"Here's your chance," Chun Wah said.

Radatan cleaned himself up as best he could. He had seen fast marches and battles recently, but here he must be a politician before he was a warrior.

The riders approached. Their ponies were like that of the Nagraks, but these men dressed somewhat differently, and they were of a taller and thinner type. Like much of what once was the Cheng empire, these people were now called Nagraks after the larger tribe around them, but once they were something else.

Radatan turned to Chun Wah. "I'm going to take a risk now. This might be done without fighting, and if I can achieve that Shar will be pleased. I hope to go into the town and talk to the elders. You're in charge of the army now. Whether I live or not, am held hostage or not, one way or another take this town for Shar."

The former monk nodded, and made a strange gesture with his fingers that Radatan had learned the people of Skultic used as an invocation of good luck.

He would need it.

Quickly he picked a half dozen men, and moved forward to meet the outcoming delegation. He wished Chun Wah could come with him, but if something happened he needed an experienced warrior here to lead the army.

They walked part way down the river embankment. Even the road was difficult in places, being steep and slippery. Bringing an army through here, all the while subject to missile attack from above would be a dangerous mission. Not impossible, but the casualties would be high.

The riders drew up before them in silence. Their ponies were sure-footed, and waited now, ears pricked. They sensed the mood of their riders.

"Who are you, and what do you wish in Tashkar?" one of the men asked.

Radatan studied him a moment. He was no warrior, at least had not been for a long time. He was middle aged, and tending toward being overweight. The sword at his side had jewels on the hilt, but that did not mean he did not know how to use it.

"I am an envoy of Shar Fei. Nakatath has sent me to negotiate."

The other man studied him in turn. "Why does she send an army if she only wishes to talk?"

Radatan assumed a look of puzzlement, and looked back at his men.

"Them? An army? No, they are but a small part of her force that come with me as a guard. These are troubled times."

It was a gamble. This man and this town would have heard rumor of Shar's army to the west. They might even know the numbers. But maybe they did not, and either way they could not be sure. It was a kind of veiled threat, if very polite as far as those things went. It meant we wish to talk rather than attack, but we have the numbers to overwhelm you if required.

The other man looked at him shrewdly. He was not a warrior, or at least had not been such for a long time, but there was a hardness to his gaze.

"Of Shar Fei we have learned. Of the Nagraks we know plenty. Both have armies. We are farmers though, and all we want is to tend our crops and run our business. Anyone who interferes with that will soon learn that while we are few, we are prepared."

The man spoke as if the people of Tashkar did not consider themselves Nagraks. He too, just as Radatan had done, offered a veiled threat, if less precise than Radatan's.

There was an opportunity in his words though. "Your business is selling grain?"

The man did not answer immediately. "It is."

He was not going to make this easy. Or quick. Radatan did not blame him. He was giving himself time to judge the character of those he faced.

"As you say, Shar has an army. And so do the Nagraks. Soldiers need feeding though, and Shar has wealth enough to buy your grain. She has no desire to fight for it."

The man grinned a little. "Well, that's an interesting proposition. The Nagraks already buy our grain though. We need no other buyers."

Radatan nodded thoughtfully. The opening he saw was there, and it had just widened. But he had traded enough horses in his time to know not to look eager.

"No doubt the Nagraks will buy your grain. And always have. But now they have competition. It may be that Shar is willing to pay a greater fee than the Nagraks. She has the money for it. Something more would be required in turn though."

"More?"

"Yes. Shelter for our army over the remaining winter."

The other man looked at him steadily with those hard eyes, giving nothing away of his thoughts. Evidently, he had heard enough though to make some kind of a decision.

"I'm just a messenger, and these are matters above my station. However, I'm authorized to lead you into the town to talk with the elders."

Radatan studied the man, and his silent companions. Could he trust them? If he went into the town would he ever come out again?

He also thought this was a delaying tactic for negotiations. No doubt one of these men would be sent into the town ahead to give word to the elders of what had been discussed. They would have time to devise a negotiation strategy before he even spoke to them.

It was not possible to know if he should trust these men. He did not feel any alarm at them though. They seemed as Cheng were the land over. Wary of strangers, set in their own customs and looking for a way to earn a living.

"Very well. Let's go and talk to the elders. If we can, it would be good to come to an arrangement before Shar arrives."

The other man grinned. He understood that was part of the bargaining. It was added pressure, but he ignored it.

"Follow us then. Take care, for the path is very difficult."

Radatan suppressed a laugh. The other man gave as good as he got. That was his way of saying that Shar, or anyone else, would struggle to take Tashkar if it came to battle, and that many would die.

He was right. For both their sides, Radatan hoped an agreement could be reached. Not just before Shar arrived, but before the Nagraks. They would be here very soon, and faster than Shar.

Radatan and his small group followed after the ponies. As he had seen from above, the road was narrow and difficult. It dropped down low into where the middle of the river once ran. The rocks were moist here, and it seemed underground water still seeped up from time to time. That moisture was frozen slick now.

The ponies scrambled over it almost effortlessly. Radatan took his time. He did not wish to fall, for he knew he was watched from above. It would not be dignified, and would hinder negotiation. It would be proof of how difficult an attack on this place would be.

Either side of the track the ground was rough and treacherous. He studied it closely. His army might yet be asked to traverse that, and it was well to scrutinize it.

Chen Fei had known his business. Radatan did not doubt that the emperor had planned these defenses out himself, and that they had been maintained through the long years.

Men would die here before a single arrow was loosed or a spear cast. Rocks would give way, and soldiers would fall and crack their heads on others. Ankles and legs would break. Gravel and sand would slide, bringing death in the form of large rocks toppling down the slopes.

Higher up were boulders. They looked secure, but Radatan did not doubt they would be rigged so as to tumble down on an army and bring an avalanche with them.

He hardened his heart. Shar would pay a premium for grain and shelter. She had the gold. But if it were not offered he must take this place for her and hold it against the Nagraks until she arrived. That he would do, no matter the cost.

He smiled after a time when a single rider went ahead of the rest.

"To bring word of your coming to the elders," the leader said. Radatan knew it was to report the words spoken earlier though, and to give the elders time to consider how best to negotiate.

After a difficult passage, they came to the portcullis. This Radatan studied with great care. It was of slabs of oak, reinforced and bound by bars of iron as thick as his leg. The end rested on an upthrust of hard stone, and under it was a kind of cavern. No doubt that was a death trap, and water, missiles and boulders could be rolled through it.

The other end entered a cave. All along the exposed cliff face were more caves. The city was one of rocky caverns, yet it seemed the only way in or out was via the portcullis. And if it were taken, even the mouth of the cave beyond was a good defense. It was narrow, enabling a small group of men to hold it. Meanwhile, caves opened above it from which more projectiles could be used to devastating effect.

The riders halted here, sorting out an order to ride one at a time over the portcullis. Several could pass abreast, but Radatan understood the purpose of doing it this way. It was to slow the procession down and give him time to study the defenses.

This was supposed to deter him from contemplating any attack. To an extent, it did. However, for Shar he would do so, and he would find a way to overcome all obstacles. It did not matter that it would be difficult. All that mattered was that it could be done, if the attackers had courage. This they did, and in the end there was no such thing as a defense that could not be beaten.

It was dark in the entrance of the cave, and the clatter of the hooves of the ponies was loud. This area was kept dark for a reason. No doubt there were further defenses here that the town elders did not wish him to see.

They passed through a long passage, and then came to a wide cavern. This was well-lit, and many torches flickered red light over the walls.

Out of side halls boys came to take the ponies of the men and led them away. No doubt there would be a system of caves near the entrance used as underground stables. It was an idea that Radatan marveled at. Nothing had gone unconsidered in this place, and his respect for the old emperor intensified. But he served she who would become the new one, and he knew she was as gifted as her forefather.

The group soon descended several long halls that ran downward, and at times stepped down steep staircases cut into the stone. These were well worn, the middle of the treads showing a depression from the wear of countless feet over countless centuries.

The place seemed old to Radatan. It was not like a forest that might be more ancient by far. A forest was a place of life and constant change, following the cycles of the year. This place was unchanging. No doubt Chen Fei, if he saw it now, would recognize everything and think but a day had passed here rather than a thousand years.

At length they came to a chamber, well-lit in which a stone table occupied the center. Around it sat a group of men, most old. Certainly they were well dressed, and most wore rings of gold. These, Radatan knew at once, were the town elders.

He did not like the looks of them. He did not dislike them either though. They were just different from the type of leaders that he knew.

The elders stood. "Welcome to Tashkar," the eldest of them said. He was taller than most, and very thin. He had a long silver beard, fine and neatly trimmed. His eyes were dark though, and despite his age there was great intelligence behind them. He was one who would detect lies and bravado quickly, and Radatan knew what his approach must be. Simply the truth.

8. Why End There?

Shar headed her army. She set the pace, and though she had started as a scout on the overgrown trails of Tsarin Fen, and was used to swift marches, she kept her strides to a slower tempo than she could.

Her army was large. It was made up of different tribes getting used to one another. There were injured warriors from previous battles, and most of all they carried a high burden of supplies. It had to be so, for they were striking out onto the Fields of Rah, and a winter snow storm or attack by enemy forces could separate them from their supply lines to the Skultic Mountains and the Nahlim Forest.

If she were the enemy, it was those very supply lines she would attack and thereby starve the army that ventured onto the plains. If she considered it, the Nagraks would too. The strategy came with risk though. To send forces to do that was to have less with which to defend Nagrak City. It was not her destination, but they did not know that. They would fear it though, and must make plans to stop it. If she took the city, she did not need supply lines.

Tashkar offered her the same benefit. With luck, they would not consider that though. It was much smaller than Nagrak City, and not a target of military significance. Except for the grain they had, and that it was a defensible position she could hold and try to link up with Kubodin. She had done all she could though to make it appear her plan was otherwise, and whatever spies were in the camp, and surely there must be some, would be reporting misinformation.

Her thoughts settled on Radatan. He was a good man, and she trusted him with her life. He was shrewd, canny and determined. His leadership had never been tested though, and that worried her.

Even so, he was a warrior born, as were all the Two Ravens Clan, and she knew he watched her closely, studied her ways and had learned from her tactics.

Her army must go slower than the smaller one she had entrusted him with, but her own still moved at a fair pace. Not fast enough to surprise the enemy, maybe, but enough to make good ground.

It was possible the enemy might miss Radatan's smaller force, and that their scouts would be concentrating on her. It was possible, but she gave the prospect little hope.

They came to the Ngar River, and grudgingly turned south following the trail and markers left by Radatan. The river was a barrier to her, but it was pretty to look at, iced over and with the branches of the trees by its banks bare of leaves and stark against the white.

Not long after a scout returned, and it was not one of her own but one of Radatan's.

"The enemy has been sighted," the man reported. "And there may be battle."

Shar did not like that, but it was expected. Much depended on what size the Nagrak force was. If it were too large, Radatan would retreat to join with her. If so, she would see him soon.

If he could retreat. The Nagraks had the advantage of being mounted. A kind of advantage anyway. It had disadvantages too, which Radatan had seen exploited. She did not fear for his force in battle. They were good men and tested. What worried her was that the shamans might have deduced her target despite all her misdirection, and sent an army too big for Radatan to fight or retreat from. If the enemy could, they would destroy his force before she arrived, and then turn toward her.

They made the river crossing as the afternoon waned. The long shadows of the few trees along the banks darkened the ice as they moved across it. They did so slowly, and with great care.

Shar ordered it done in stages. First, the scouts reported that no enemy was close. Then a third of the army crossed. Those who knew about such things then inspected the ice carefully.

It was declared safe. Another third crossed, and they repeated the procedure. Then the last of the army came over. By that time a camp had been established. Earth ramparts were thrown up, a perimeter of scouts and sentries was established. Latrine trenches were dug and cooking fires started.

There was little timber available for fires. However, the dried dung of cattle and horses was used as well, of which there was plenty if foraging expeditions were made beyond the fertile flood plain of the river.

Shar had done all she could to be ready for an attack. One might come soon, for she was in the heart of enemy territory now.

There was no sign of the enemy though, and the fires seemed cozy in the gathering dark and the warm food enriched the souls of her warriors. There was nothing quite like a campfire and a warm meal after a hard day's work.

"Let them enjoy it while they can," she said to Asana.

The swordmaster, always by her side as though he feared an assassination attempt, looked around him.

"It will be different tomorrow. At the very least it will be a hard march, but likely there'll be battle. For once, you cannot have caught the enemy by surprise."

"No, but let's hope that Radatan has. So much depends on his mission."

Asana grinned. He knew now what Shar planned, and he approved. He at least she trusted, and she knew he would tell no one.

There was a meeting that night around a campfire. Timber was in short supply, and it was not much of a fire. It gave off little warmth and much smoke, for the timber was damp with snow and still had sap in it. There was little deadwood to be found.

The chiefs liked the smoke though. The breath of the gods they said, and it did not seem to matter how far she journeyed they all thought that. She had seen gods though, and knew better. To her, it was just a smell that clung to her cloak the next day and lingered in her hair.

"Is there no word yet from Radatan?" Boldgrim asked.

There was not. It disturbed the chiefs, but not Shar. He would send word when he could. Probably he had encountered the enemy, and them being Nagraks on horseback he thought it prudent not to waste the lives of scouts who could be outrun. Perhaps overnight he would risk sending some, under the cover of dark. If so, she would still not likely hear any news until the march began again tomorrow.

"Radatan knows how to look after himself," she said. "And he has five thousand men. Give him time. He'll take Tashkar, one way or another."

The night grew old around them, and the camp quieted down as the soldiers slept. One by one the chiefs drifted away, and only Huigar was left. Now that

Radatan was gone, she took her role as bodyguard even more seriously.

Shar was not tired. Her mind was too full of things. Possibilities. Plans. Contingencies. Fears. But at length she went to her own tent, took off her boots and found a blanket to wrap herself in.

The swords of Dawn and Dusk she kept close to hand, one to each side of her so that no matter which direction she rolled to in her sleep one or the other would always be within easy reach.

It was cold in the tent, and she tossed and turned pulling her blankets close and her hood up. Huigar, sleeping in the tent entrance, so that anyone coming in must wake her, seemed troubled also.

Sleep came slowly, but when it did it pulled her deep. She dreamed of many things, and then it seemed to her that her dreams changed to reality even though she knew it was not so.

She strode at the head of her army, and it was winter no more but high summer. The multitudes of her soldiers were numerous as the grass heads on the plain, for she had joined at last with Kubodin and other tribes from the perimeter of the Cheng lands had come to her also.

She turned and gazed behind her. The Fields of Rah were not green any more, but red. The blood of the Nagraks and shamans wetted it, and the noon sun sent crimson gleams splintering back up into the sky.

The war was won. She was victorious. Soon she would be crowned empress, and all the Cheng would bow to her, and all the vast lands of the empire would be hers to rule.

"Why end there," a voice whispered in her dreams.

"What else is there? This is my destiny. This is my purpose. For this I was born – to overthrow the tyrants. To destroy the shamans and rid the world of their evil."

"It is one good deed, in truth. But a small one. Very small, Shar Fei. Were you not born for more than this?"

"What do you mean?"

"Do you think evil exists only in the Cheng Empire? Truly, all Alithoras is under its sway. There are nations you have never heard of, in lands you can but dream of, where they are subjected to tyranny even as your own small nation. Will you not rise to help them?"

Shar felt the pull of that. It was like a fire that caught in her mind, and in moments leaped up into a raging inferno. She had lived under tyranny all her life, even as a child. Had the clan's shaman known her ancestry he would have killed her. It was intolerable.

And others lived like that. They faced the same hardships. They were not called slaves, and they might think they were free. In reality though, they toiled for others. For an elite class who lied to them. Deceived them. Told them they offered protection when they themselves were the threat.

Her mind seemed to reach out. It was still a dream, but it was real too. Over the land she swept. Grasslands and rivers flickered by. Over mountains her thought reached, and she knew the long chain of them that she saw were the Eagle Claw Mountains. To the left one mountain brooded, rising higher than the others and casting a great shadow. Three Moon Mountain. It sent a chill through her, but she did not know why.

Then she was beyond. Beyond into foreign lands. Lakes and rivers she saw as they swept by ever more swiftly, then afar the sea.

Down the coast she sped, and she saw great cities. She sensed magic, but she did not know how. One young king glanced up at her from the horse he rode, and she felt hatred stir inside her. Here was an enemy!

There was doubt too. The glance he gave was clear-sighted and firm. She sensed curiosity. She sensed he knew she was there, but he did not attack. It might be that he was not her enemy, but the enemy of the force on which she rode, that sped her over the land.

Then the young man was gone. Other cities swept up, some still recovering from the signs of war. Conflict was everywhere. The need for help was everywhere.

Another range of mountains lifted up to the south. Behind them she sensed great power. Great magic. And…

And her flight blurred. The land dissolved away below her and she was back in her tent in the camp of her army.

A cold sweat sleeked her body. She stood, and in her hands were the swords of Dawn and Dusk. She had no memory of drawing them.

9. Almost a Ghost

Shulu held the man's hand in one of her own, and gently palpated it with the other. He made no noise, nor even winced, but his breath quickened.

She did not need that sign to know severe damage had been done. It was likely more than a bad sprain, and weighing everything up she thought one of the many small bones had been broken. The man's capacity to endure pain was high, and she admired him. It would not change the outcome though.

She glanced into the warrior's eyes, and she saw that he knew. Her duty of care was to him, but she was in the shaman's employ, and he stood close by, watching. She did not like it, but she spoke to him first. That was what he expected.

"The wrist has a broken bone. I'll apply a splint, and some herbs to help with the pain, but he'll need to rest it for six weeks. And then it will take quite some time to regain proper strength and movement."

The shaman grunted. He did that a lot, and it set Shulu's nerves on edge. Speak, and say something intelligent. Or hold your silence and think. Grunting was for pigs. But she kept that view to herself and smoothed over her expression.

"A trainee nazram with a broken wrist is no good to me. He still eats the same, injured or uninjured. That's a waste of time and money."

Shulu shrugged. "It is what it is. The way these men train, injuries will occur. You push them to be good, and that comes at a price."

64

"It does. But I'm tired of paying it. Send him back to his village. He can try to join the nazram again another time."

Out of the corner of her eye she saw the disappointment on the young man's face. Misguided as he was, he thought this a good thing and likely the chance might not come again once lost.

The shaman turned to go, but Shulu stopped him. "If you let him go now, you've lost everything you put in so far."

He narrowed his eyes at her. No one ever questioned his decisions, and he was trying to decide if she just had.

"So what if his right wrist is damaged? He has a left one, doesn't he? He can learn to wield a sword with that. A man that can fight with either hand is rare, and in the end he'll be better than the others."

The shaman pursed his lips. "Maybe," he said.

Shulu pushed it a little further. "It won't be easy for him. He'll have a harder time of it than the rest. That's good. It'll save him from being weak like some of the others who glide through without problems."

"You seem to know a lot about fighting. What makes you think he can learn to wield a sword with his left hand?"

Shulu lied quickly. "I saw a man do it once. His wrist wasn't broken. His hand was mauled by a dog and the tendons damaged. He never did get the use of it back, but he learned to hold a sword in his left hand, and do near everything else with it too. Better than most folks who use both hands. It stuck with me, and I know it can be done."

The shaman grunted again, this time directing his words to the young warrior.

"All right. You can stay for now. But I'll be watching."

The shaman strode away and Shulu watched him from behind. He was so arrogant, and so annoying. He was a shaman though, and that was their type. It came in part from their training, and in part from the use of magic. Both set them aside from others, and gave a sense of superiority.

All things were relative however. And she felt about him as he did to mere warriors. It was a fault, and she knew it.

The supplies she needed were close to hand, for this was not the first injury in the training yard. She began to place the wrist in a splint, and looked over her shoulder to make sure the shaman was gone. He was, but in the shadows under the mansion close by she saw the witch-woman watching her.

That old woman was the bane of her existence, and Shulu muttered under her breath.

"I'm sorry, I didn't hear that," the warrior asked.

She glanced back at him. "Never mind. I was just talking to myself. Old women do that."

Regrettably, she could not use magic to relieve the man's pain. At least, it was not worth the risk. There was something about the witch-woman that made her more than she seemed. She might guess, or observe, or have knowledge of magic greater than her actual inherent power with it, and it was best after all that had happened recently for Shulu to do nothing more to draw attention to herself.

The wrist was firmly bound. She gave the man instructions on how to use the herbs she handed to him at the same time, and made him repeat back her directions.

"Good," she said. "And how are you with your left hand, anyway?"

"Terrible." He looked suddenly determined. "But I'll learn."

"Yes you will. It'll be hard at first, but the more you persist the quicker it will come to you."

She let him go then and watched the rest of the training going on around her. Many men were sparring, and wooden swords and steel swords clashed together. The wooden swords gave less injuries. The steel swords, even without an edge, could be extremely damaging. Yet learning to fight really was a tough task, and the harder their training was now the greater their chances of surviving battle later.

The witch-woman came out of the shadows, a slight sneer on her face. Or maybe that was her natural expression.

"You always have slick replies to the shaman's questions."

Shulu felt her hatred stir, but tried as best she could to keep it under control.

"The truth is quick to some tongues. Venom to others."

It was not subtle, nor was it intended to be. It could have been a much harsher comment though, and Shulu was pleased that she had held herself in check when her natural instincts cried out for far, far more.

The other woman merely grinned, as though she knew something but would not say, and walked easily away. It was not the reaction Shulu expected, and it worried her. Perhaps it had just been for show. Or maybe the witch-woman had a trick yet to play.

By the time the nazram in training stopped for the noon rest and to get something to eat, rumor was abroad in the mansion. Shulu heard it first from a maid, then one of the cook's helpers and finally from a man delivering supplies. Shar Fei was on the march, the rumor claimed. She was heading toward Nagrak City.

Each time Shulu pretended to be surprised. Each time she tried to draw out what the person knew without seeming to have a special interest. That was not hard because everyone was talking about it and discussing, at length, what it meant and what would happen next.

No one knew more than the basic information though. No one had seen her army first hand, or met with a warrior who had. It was all hearsay.

She ate a quick lunch with the other servants in the communal dining hall. Of the witch-woman, there was no sign. The place was rowdy, for the talk of Shar caught on like a wildfire. Every conversation at every table was about it, but there was nothing new.

The food was good in the shaman's mansion. They lived better here than some chiefs did in the poorer communities. Shulu ate very little though. She had a few spoonfuls of soup and some crusty bread. There were other dishes, but she ignored them. Of late, she had no hunger. Perhaps for years she had not eaten a hearty meal. She just had no appetite anymore, and that was yet another sign of her extreme age.

She was almost a ghost. There was no flesh on her bones, and death was her constant companion. *Not yet, you old bastard. Not until Shar is victorious and Chen avenged.*

Talking to oneself was not a good sign either. But she had one last task to accomplish in her life, and she would achieve it even if she truly became a ghost. Nothing would stop her.

What was Shar thinking though? It was too soon to march on Nagrak City. She should be joining up with Kubodin. There was strength in great numbers, and only a vast army could hope to conquer the Nagraks. Or the shamans, once they went to war. If a final battle loomed,

68

and if they were under threat, they would gather from all corners of the old empire and come down from Three Moon Mountain in wrath. Cowards they might be at times, but a cornered coward was the most dangerous sort of enemy. They could strike out unpredictably. They could show the greatest of courage, if but for a little while.

Unless...

Yes. It might be a subterfuge.

The more she thought about that, the more likely it seemed. And a good one too, for even *she* had considered it as reality. Yet if so, what was her true goal? And what could be done in Nagrak City to help her?

10. The Dragon's Breath

Lunch was over, and so was Shulu's break. She went back down to the training yard and took a seat on one of the benches. She had to be on hand in case of an accident, but the men were only coming back from their own lunch. She should have a little while to think before she was needed.

She turned the idea of subterfuge over in her mind. Whichever way she looked at it, the idea fit. She knew Shar as well as Shar knew herself. How often had they played such games of tactics and strategies. *If this happened, what would you do? If the enemy does such and such, how would you counter it?* Games they had been, and enjoyable. But also a learning experience. Whatever Shar *seemed* to be doing now, it would be the opposite.

That could really only mean one thing. If Nagrak City was not her target, it would be joining up with Kubodin. Nothing else made sense, and yet that would not be easy. Not easy at all, for winter usually hit the Fields of Rah hard, and there would be no shelter from the cold. Men would die and sicken. The rest would be weak when they reached Chatchek Fortress, and there they would face battle.

Shulu suddenly smiled. She understood now. Shar intended something else. She would seek shelter over winter, and yet make it look like an attack. If the enemy believed it was Nagrak City, all the better. If they saw through her outer plan, and decided she wanted to join Kubodin, that was fine too. Her real plan, her innermost thought, would be to protect her army as best she could.

To keep them strong for the summer of fighting to come. That was not far off, so she would take Tashkar. It held supplies. It was a fortress designed by Chen himself, and that would appeal to her. It had come up in the never-ending discussions of her youth. And from there, come spring, she could still keep the Nagraks guessing her intention even after her initial subterfuge had been laid bare.

If Shar could join with Kubodin her army would be massive. They could then ring Nagrak City and tighten around it like a noose. It would mean bloody battle after bloody battle, but with luck she could take the city. She would be empress then. Only the shamans would defy her, as they had defied Chen, from Three Moon Mountain.

They would always be a threat. They would always be a splinter in Shar's skin, annoying her and threatening infection. There was a way to deal with that. Prophecy had shown it to Shulu long ago, but the way it unfolded was unclear. So was the when. There was much of the future she could not read, but she had taken precautions…

Enough of that. She must deal with the problem at hand. She surveyed the men training around her, and all seemed as it should. There was time yet to think.

If Shar wanted to make Nagrak City, and the shamans, think they would soon be under siege the best thing to do was to further that idea. And by good fortune, or fate, Shulu was in just the right spot to help.

Many of her spies were in Nagrak City. She had not heard from them of late, but it was time to reestablish contact. She might learn things of value from them, but they were not just spies. They were agents of influence too. She could use that to great advantage now.

The afternoon wore on, and she was called several times to help warriors with minor injuries. Nothing taxed her skill greatly. She had been healing such injuries all her life, and that was a very, very long time.

The shadows of dusk eventually spilled over the yard, and then night came. Once more she went to the communal dining room, and made a show of eating. She could barely wait to leave though. She had a plan now, and speed was required.

The meal ended, and some people began to leave. She forced herself to wait a little longer so as not to give anyone reason to think this night would be different to her than any other.

At last she returned her plate to a counter where the used crockery was left, and then walked out from the hall behind a larger group. She headed toward her own room, but once she was sure she was alone she changed direction and slipped out a little used exit onto the main street at the front of the mansion.

She pulled her hood up to hide her identity, and she walked with a brisker stride than she used in the mansion. If someone saw her they would not likely recognize her, especially in the dark. With that in mind, she walked down the middle of the street and further away from the burning torches that lined the footpath at regular intervals.

The street was still crowded, and that was good. She was just one more person hustling along and no one had any reason to pay attention to her. Here, in the city, no one wanted to anyway. In a village, if you met someone coming the other way you would stop and talk to them even if you hated them. Here, in this era, many people would walk past you if you had fallen and injured yourself, pretending they had not noticed.

The world had changed since her youth. What would it be like in another thousand years? That was someone else's problem. It was enough for her to deal with the time in which she lived, and that time was drawing to a close.

She would not be sad to go. All she wanted before then was to see Shar victorious and to avenge Chen. Nothing else mattered. Not anymore.

Her destination took her closer to the palace. Closer to the place where Chen had been murdered. The streets had changed in all the years she had been away, but here and there she recognized a building or an intersection. Fortunately, she was not in sight of the palace nor would be.

The houses were rich. Most were mansions like the shaman's, but not quite as big. Immense wealth was on display everywhere. She passed manicured gardens lit by lamps of colored glass, small waterfalls and man-made creeks over which arched bridges of ornately carved timber spanned. It was all foolishness.

Chen had liked colored lamps like that though. Once he had even…

Shulu stopped herself. Now was not the time to think of Chen. If her anger rose she might find the nearest shaman and burn him to ashes with the wrath of her magic. And when the others came she would destroy them, until at last she was overcome. No. Best not to think of him just now. Not until her task was complete and she had fulfilled the revenge in her heart that had been nurtured years beyond count.

The corner ahead was one she recognized. It was a shopping district, and here there were no mansions but various businesses such as leatherworkers, smiths and establishments that sold clothes.

None of those was her destination though. When she came to the corner she hesitated, making sure that she was not being followed. There was movement behind her somewhere in the shadows, but people were coming and going, if fewer here than on the streets further back. She turned left and continued.

This was an area that had changed more than the rest of the city. There was nothing that she recognized, and the foot traffic was suddenly a lot less. No doubt during the day it was busy. At night, less people had cause to come this way.

She found the place she was looking for sooner than expected. It was a better building for the street than most, if smaller, and it had a sign at the front, magnificently carved in wood with tendrils coming up from it of twisted strands of timber that suggested smoke. *The Dragon's Breath Inn* the sign proclaimed.

It was a joke. It was a reference to herself, for one of her epithets was the Dragon of the Empire. It was she, in popular belief, who guarded the land and protected it. If only the people knew how limited her power was.

She paused in the shadows. There were few people on the street, and those she saw seemed slightly worried. As well they would be, thinking an army was approaching to invade. She wanted to see more than that though. She wanted to see fear. Panic even. That would set a fire amongst the shamans and the Nagrak military commanders. Such strong sentiments in the city might precipitate a false step. It might lead them into errors of judgement that Shar could seize upon.

There was no indication that anyone had followed her or paid her any attention at all. That was well. She turned briskly, crossed the street and entered through the double doors, curved at the tops to suggest a cave. A dragon's lair.

She smiled as she entered. It was she who had designed this place long ago, and the name, sign and doors were her idea. The inn turned a tidy profit, year after year and was one of her better ventures. It had been a good decision to buy the building and open the inn. Both in terms of income and as a means of spying. What better place than an inn where strangers came and went, and were expected to do so without suspicion? And what better way to loosen tongues than by a glass, or several, of beer?

It was warm inside and well-lit. It was cheery. Even so, she could not shake off the feeling that she was taking a risk to come here. It was run by one of her spies, but if her disguise had been seen through, she would bring suspicion onto the place just by being here.

11. Difficult Choices

Radatan was seated at a table with the elders, and the men he had brought with him were offered chairs behind him.

"Thank you for seeing me," Radatan said, addressing his remark to those at the table but looking specifically at the old man with the silver beard.

"Did we have a choice? We wish to avoid conflict. But if it comes, we are prepared."

He was direct, and Radatan liked that. He had heard the Nagraks were high on ceremony, and this was yet another indication that those in Tashkar, while officially Nagraks, were once of a different tribe in origin.

"There are always choices, and Shar Fei wishes no conflict either. The opposite, in fact. It is the shamans who divide us. She would bring us all together as one nation, like we once were."

Radatan watched closely for a reaction to that. He would be able to see from it if they were for or against the shamans. In his travels with Shar he had met many who were against them, but would not say so until the threat of them had been removed.

"We have followed Shar's exploits," the old man said. "It might be that she can achieve her goal. But the shamans are strong. And so are the Nagraks. Nothing is certain."

It was a vague answer, and it said nothing. The elder was a skilled negotiator and would give nothing away of what he thought. Yet that revealed something, at least. He was willing to negotiate, otherwise he would have come down on the side of the shamans and be done with it.

"I'm no negotiator," Radatan said. "I speak with the full authority of Shar Fei though. And time presses. So this is what I propose."

He was giving nothing away with that. Nothing that they did not already know.

"Shar does not wish conflict. Not with you. She is generous. She has great wealth, recaptured from the shamans she has overthrown. They hoard it in secret like a dragon that lies on its heaped treasure. She will pay you for food, supplies and the use of your fortified town. She will pay you more than the shamans, and no blood will be spilled. If you are not her enemy, what could be fairer or better for you and your people than that?"

The old man leaned back in his chair thoughtfully. The other elders exchanged looks, and some whispered to each other.

"It was rude of me not to introduce myself," the old man said. "My name is Rushkatar."

It did not sound like a Nagrak name to Radatan. Nor even a Cheng one.

Radatan inclined his head in respect. "I'm pleased to meet you. Names don't really matter at the moment though. Actions do, and swift ones. That's just the facts of the situation, and I think you're one who appreciates that. You seek to give yourself time to answer my proposal. I give it. But I cannot give much. That's not in my control to give. Soon, either Shar or the Nagraks will arrive."

Rushkatar studied him. "You're an honest man, and straightforward. I like that. But the question is not just one of choices. It's also of trust. Can we rely on Shar to pay us as promised? For once she occupies the town, then she has bypassed our defenses."

"That is true." Radatan leaned forward, and he spoke from the heart. "I would die for Shar Fei. In turn, she would die for the Cheng people. You speak of trust? I can give no better testimony to her character than that. She does not seek to overthrow the shamans to take their place. She seeks to free the people from tyranny. It's not for herself that she takes on the trials she does, but for the empire that could be."

It was a grand statement. For many, it would be hollow. For Shar Fei, he believed it was the truth. Would these elders believe it though?

Rushkatar sat in silence, thinking. He was not convinced.

"There is this too," Radatan added. "You know the stories of Chen Fei, her ancestor. It was he who built this very fortress city in which we sit. The shamans say terrible things about him. Do you believe them? Or do you believe the stories passed around a campfire? Shar Fei is no different. She is his descendant, and the blood runs true even after a thousand years. In any story, does Chen Fei break his word? He doesn't. And Shar is the same. Let her into the city. Sell her what she needs, at a high profit. And should the shamans prevail, which I don't think they will, tell the Nagraks you were coerced by the presence of her army."

Radatan sat back. He had said all he could. If they did not agree, then events would be channeled into battle. His army would attempt to take this fortress, and if he did not succeed, at least it would be so weakened that Shar could sweep in.

There were several long moments of silence. The elders whispered among themselves, and Radatan could not tell what they were thinking or what decision they would make.

Rushkatar took no part in the whispered conversations. He sat apart from the rest aloof and deep in thought. After a little while he stood, and bowed to Radatan.

"You have spoken what you believe to be the truth. Now we must hold council and decide what *we* believe. We will decide within the hour. Is that acceptable?"

It was as good a hope as Radatan was going to get, and he could do no more.

"That is acceptable."

A servant was called who led Radatan and his men to a room a little way off. Refreshments were served to them, and there they rested.

"Shar will find it difficult to take this place," one of the men said.

Radatan, aware that even a stone-walled room might allow for conversations to be spied upon, answered carefully.

"Of course. The defenses are excellent. What else could be expected from Chen Fei? But she is his true descendent. If she must, she *will* take this place. Better for everyone though if the elders agree to my proposal. The gold is nothing to her. The outcome is all that counts, and she *will* have the outcome she requires, one way or another."

Time drew on, and Radatan grew anxious. The hour must nearly be up, and they had heard no word. He went to the door and opened it. Even as he did so the guard that was placed there at their service was falling. Blood blossomed over his tunic from a knife thrust, and his killer stood over him and looked up into Radatan's eyes.

They were both surprised, and neither moved for a moment. The attacker reacted first.

"Now!" he cried out, and tried to grab the door to pull it open. Radatan resisted, and even as they struggled he saw a group of soldiers come racing around the corner of the hallway, swords drawn.

If they were to live, at least for a while, they must barricade themselves inside the room. With a deft kick to the groin, Radatan sent the attacker sprawling.

He slammed the door shut. There was no lock, merely a cross board of timber that slid into a latch. He rammed it home, but it would not hold long.

"Quickly!" he called. "Push the furniture before the door!"

The soldiers reacted quickly. They did as asked, but there was not much to work with. They upended a wooden table and rammed it tight against the door even as the timber was being hammered at from the other side by kicking and shouldering. Next went some chairs. There was nothing else though.

"Traitors!" one of the soldiers cried. There was fear in his voice, as well there might be. They would all die here. A handful of men betrayed within the fortress of the enemy could not last long.

Radatan spoke in a steady voice. "Chun Wah will avenge us. He'll attack if we don't return. If we can hold on for a day or two, we might even survive."

He had to give the men some hope. It would take at least two days for Chun Wah to break inside the fortress, assuming he was not attacked by the force they had already battled with, and that would be at a heavy cost in lives. He might not do it at all. If not though, Shar would avenge them.

It soon became evident that they would not hold the attackers out for more than minutes though. Someone had an axe, and it splintered the door. The latch broke, and the door slid partially open.

The soldiers leaned against the table, using their weight to hold it in place. Radatan stabbed through the hole in the door the axe had made, and one of the enemy screamed. It had not been a killing stab, but it must have caused a terrible injury.

For a moment the beating against the door ceased, then the attack was renewed. Probably someone else had taken up the axe.

The new attacker struck, then leaped back. Several times Radatan tried to stab him, but missed. The door, however, fell apart under the assault. The attackers were now revealed, seething at the entrance and trying to break in.

Through the broken door swords jabbed, and one of the men holding the table in place reeled back, blood welling from a shoulder injury. Radatan leaped in to take his place, trying to steady the table with his bodyweight but defending himself with his sword at the same time.

A sense of desperation filled the air, for once the enemy got inside it would all be over in moments. A sword tip came close to Radatan's throat, and he felt the whisper of death breathing down his neck.

From outside there was a great clamor. Shouting rose up and the assault increased in intensity. Then it faded away.

Radatan stuck his head up over the top of the table. Through the ruined door he saw the enemy being attacked from the rear. At first, he could not see who was doing it.

"Chun Wah has come to rescue us!" one of his men said.

Radatan was not so sure. Surely Chun Wah could not possibly have got inside. Even if he could, he would not have attacked yet. It was too soon to know the outcome of negotiations.

"I don't think so," he said. "No. Those who attacked us must be rebels in Tashkar, probably nazram or under the influence of shamans. They're being brought into check by others from the town."

Radatan made up his mind. He had not liked hiding away behind a door. Now he pulled back the table and kicked down the remnants of the door. He stepped into the corridor and began laying about him with his sword. The men with him did the same, and now the situation had reversed. Those who had been about to be killed now slew, and they did so fiercely.

Many of the attackers died, and the screams filled the corridor and their blood stained the stone floor. Swiftly it became apparent that they were outmatched, being pressed from both front and rear. They surrendered, and Radatan had to order his men to stop several times, such was their anger.

The survivors of those who had attacked were quickly disarmed, and held in arm locks by warriors. Then they were marched away.

Radatan wiped the blood off his sword on the tunic of a dead man, and when he looked up the elders were approaching, led by Rushkatar.

The old man was calm, but his face was red and his lips tight as though with anger.

"Radatan," he said. "Messenger of Shar Fei. And you other men who serve her. I cannot apologize enough. This should not have happened, and the men who attacked you have no honor, nor any longer their freedom. I'm so sorry. This should not have happened."

Radatan looked at him cooly. He believed it was not sanctioned by the elders, otherwise the attack would not have been stopped. Nevertheless, his store of patience was running low.

"How did it happen?"

"We don't know yet. What was planned was transmitted to us by one who is loyal, but was held in trust by the conspirators. We believe them to be in league with our shaman."

Radatan understood what was meant. The man who had told them was a spy for them.

"And your shaman?"

"We're currently looking for him, but without luck so far."

"He's long gone," Radatan said. "Anyway, that's of no importance now. What decision have you come to?"

He was not sure his men had moved on so fast from being attacked one moment to forgetting it and going back to their task in the next. He heard their mutterings behind him. All that mattered to him though was serving Shar. And the elders were not behind the attack.

"We set a price of double the usual rate for our grain. We will allow Shar to scrutinize our records to verify that. Her army can enter the city, and fortify it. Her soldiers must fight to hold it, and not our own. The duration of the agreement will expire immediately before the next harvest. Are you, as her representative, authorized to agree to those terms?"

Radatan did not wish to appear too eager. He could afford no delay though.

"I am. And I agree in her name. She'll fulfill those terms."

Looking at the faces of the elders, he could tell this was not a unanimous decision. It was best to act now as swiftly as possible before any change of heart.

Several new men arrived, evidently being ordered to remove the dead attackers and to clean the floor of blood.

"Come then," Rushkatar said. "We must hurry."

Radatan caught a hint of urgency in his voice, and a sense of unease settled over him.

"Why?"

83

"You must return to your army and bring them into the city swiftly. If you still have time. We have just received word that Nagraks approach. They have sent a large army from Nagrak City itself, and they are nearly here."

Radatan wasted no time on useless questions. He must return to his army and act as quickly as possible. This Nagrak army might be the one he had already dealt with, but it did not sound like it. It sounded like a new one, and the two would no doubt join forces. If so, they would be too large for him.

12. You Will Die

An escort was provided for Radatan and his men, and they were given ponies to speed their traversing of the ravine before the town.

Radatan knew time was running out. He needed to be with his army, and quickly. He needed whatever news his scouts could bring. Yet even on horseback the road was difficult, and it seemed to take forever.

He leaped from his pony when he drew near to Chun Wah who came forward from the army to get to him sooner.

"The enemy approaches," the former monk said.

"I know. How large is it?"

"Larger than us. Our scouts believe it's the force we faced ourselves, in addition to a new one. It's situated itself between us and the approach Shar will take to get here."

Radatan thought quickly. He was no military commander. Not on this scale. But no one had been for a thousand years. The facts were simple enough though. He could bring his troops into the town, and they had enough, more than enough, to hold it against the enemy. That must be done. Even so, Shar would be driving straight toward the Nagrak force. She would not divert or back away. Who knew what other Nagrak reinforcements were on the way though?

That meant a battle was coming, and the numbers were not so much in Shar's favor that Radatan was comfortable with leaving her to fend for herself. And given the speed of mounted Nagrak forces, the situation could worsen quickly.

He glanced at Chun Wah. "We have an agreement with the town. Take the army and enter. Do it quickly."

"And you?"

"I'll call for five hundred volunteers. We'll distract the Nagraks. We'll be a thorn in their side. We must unsettle them so they cannot face Shar on ground of their choosing. If we lose her, or her army, the rebellion is lost."

"Five hundred men is not enough," Chun Wah said.

"We'll *make* it enough." Radatan said. "For Shar. Now go. Go quickly. The elders can be trusted, but know there are elements in the city that cannot. Keep your eyes open."

Radatan marched over the Fields of Rah. Scouts reported to him the movement of the enemy, and he and his volunteers headed straight at them. It was a mission that would end in death. He knew it, and he made sure the volunteers understood it also. Their task was not to live, but to survive long enough to disrupt the Nagraks, and to divide their attention.

He was proud of the men. They did not fight for themselves, or their tribe. They fought for the empire that could be, free of the tyranny of shamans.

One thing was to their advantage, and he must use it as best as possible. The enemy would not believe that such a small force would dare to challenge them. They would fear a greater force being held in reserve. They would fear being led into a trap. And if their own scouts reported that no such force existed, at worst that would take time. At best, they may not believe those reports. Why should they? It would not make any sense.

All Radatan needed was time. If he could delay the enemy by half a day, maybe even a full day, it would be enough. Shar could fight them then close to Tashkar with a better chance of victory and reinforcement. The enemy might even retreat, fearing being caught between two armies.

In any event, he sent word to Shar via several of his scouts. He was careful to make his message obscure, both about securing Tashkar and about his efforts in the field, lest any of the scouts be captured. But Shar would understand his message.

It was not long before the two forces drew close together. Radatan had a parley flag made and signaled with it. The enemy ignored him, riding forward in a steady trot. He could not blame them, for he had done the same thing himself.

He too kept marching. His men formed a tight square, and he angled them across the approaching front. It was a strange tactic. Even a bizarre one. For that reason it had its intended effect. The enemy, unsure of what was happening, drew to a stop.

"Quickly!" Radatan commanded the soldier near him who had a horn used for signaling. "Sound a retreat."

The message was given to the column, and they neatly turned and marched away from the Nagrak riders. Radatan set a slow pace. He did not want the enemy thinking they were retreating in fear.

He studied the Nagraks over his shoulder as his men marched. The enemy were confounded, and no doubt feared they were being led into a trap.

Did they know of Shar's army approaching? He must assume they did. What he was doing though made it look as though he was trying to lead them into an ambush. Judging from their reaction, they thought exactly that.

Eventually the riders came forward at a trot. Even as they did so Radatan gave an order and his force changed direction, moving at a right angle and toward a long hill that sloped gracefully over the Fields of Rah. It was hardly high ground, but it was high enough that an army might be hidden behind it.

No doubt the enemy scouts had passed through that area. Yet the commander must believe what he saw with his own two eyes. Everything Radatan was doing had the hallmarks of attempting to lead him into a trap. Despite the intelligence he must have, he was wary.

Radatan came to the crest of the slope. There he halted and turned back to face the enemy. If they attacked, the horses must run up hill. The Nagraks would not like that. If they went to the rear to attack the ambush they feared, it would take them time. And Radatan would still hold the high ground. It was not enough advantage to make any real difference, but he would use whatever advantage, no matter how small, as best he could.

The enemy was in doubt. It hesitated, as those in doubt do. Radatan knew it could not last, but he had gained the attention of the commander and prevented him from concentrating on Shar. If he even knew of her presence. For if he did, he had now been maneuvered out of her direct path to Tashkar.

"They will come soon," he said to his men. "Doubt does not last forever."

He was not eager to be proved correct. An hour passed, and still the enemy did not come. Then at last, no doubt based on repeated assurances from returning mounted scouts that no greater force lay behind the one on the crest of the slope, they moved in to crush those who had dared to confront them.

Radatan had a spear, and he held it up slowly. "You know what to do," he cried out. And his force was small enough that all might hear him. "Stand firm. Use your spears. To flee is to die. Above all, remember that what we do now is for Shar, and for the free empire she will build."

At first the only noise was the rolling trot of the ponies as they ascended the gentle slope. Then the men began to chant, and Radatan felt a thrill run through his body.

Shar Fei! Shar Fei! Shar Fei! they called.

And he called out with them. He knew her better than they did, but they loved her just as much. Suddenly, he felt that nothing could stop her. For who she was, and what she did, the people loved her.

No one ever chanted the names of the shamans. Shar would triumph over them, and complete what her ancestor had been assassinated to prevent. Their destruction.

The riders came on. They drew close to the front rank of spearmen, and wheeled sideways using their curved swords to slash. It was not very effective. More of them died by far than Radatan's men. Even so, the Nagraks outnumbered them by so much that it did not matter.

Some of the riders continued around the square, and soon all four sides were under attack. Men died, and others in the inner ranks took hold of their spears and assumed their place.

There was no chanting now. There was just brutal fighting as the Nagraks made one pass after another. The square grew smaller.

Radatan considered what to do. There was nothing better than this though. To move was to give up the high ground, which small advantage as it was still offered some help.

The Nagraks fought with fury. Some of these men had been defeated before, and they had learned to fear the spears of Shar's soldiers. In this situation though, even if some of them died, each pass killed their enemy, and the square kept shrinking.

The dead left behind were trampled by the horses. It was horrible to see, and Radatan sensed his own death drawing near.

So be it. No man lived forever, and his death served a purpose. Only half his force remained, and it would disintegrate quickly now. The men who yet lived grew tired, and the shadow of death fell over the fragment of their force that was left.

"For Shar!" he called out. He was surprised to hear the deep-throated response of his men take up his call. They would die with him now, but their belief in the emperor would outlive them.

The fighting wore on. They were down to a hundred men now, but they had drawn out their deaths far longer than Radatan would have thought possible. The best fighters were left, and their skill and determination to sell their lives dearly wreaked havoc among the enemy.

It was late in the afternoon. Radatan's men would not live to see the dusk, but suddenly a horn blew in the midst of the enemy riders and they withdrew. They gathered in one place a little below the crest of the slope that Radatan held, and there they assembled quietly.

Out of the midst of the enemy a single rider came. Expertly, he guided his pony up the slope, avoiding fallen Nagraks, dead ponies and lastly the bodies of Radatan's own men.

Radatan stepped forward from the ranks of his men. He still held his spear, but he used it as a staff to help him stand up. His legs ached. His shoulders throbbed. And he felt more tired than ever in his life.

The enemy gazed at him from atop his horse. "You fight well."

Radatan felt an afternoon breeze pick up, and it blew cold across his sweaty and blood-caked face.

"We fight for freedom. It gives us strength."

"And yet you will die. So I say this to you, surrender, and tell us what you know of Shar Fei's plans, and I will let you live. Even to walk free."

Radatan studied the man carefully. He was obviously the leader, and of higher rank than the one Radatan had met with before. He had sent no messenger but come himself, and it was a mark of respect. Nor did he seem untrustworthy. His gaze was steady, and he was a man such as Radatan had met often. He was a true warrior, and he fought because that was what he was commanded to do. He did not hate his enemy. He did what was required, and that done, he would leave his enemy in peace. Even respect them, if they had fought well as Radatan's men had done.

He turned around and looked from side to side at his men.

"Do you hear that? We are offered our lives if we surrender. If I, who know a little of Shar Fei's plans, reveal them. What do you say?"

There was a heavy silence. The chance of life had been offered, and many wanted that. Yet not at a cost to Shar. For himself, he would let the men decide. In truth, he did not know anything of what Shar intended beyond the capture of Tashkar. She had said things, but he had learned that what she said was often a subterfuge. They would learn nothing of value from him except that.

One man called out. "Kill all the shamans! Shar Fei is our hero, and we'll not betray her."

Radatan lifted his hands high. "Speak truthfully! Is this the answer of you all? Do any disagree?"

His answer was silence. None disagreed, and he felt a surge of pride in his men. They had lost this battle, but they had won a far greater victory.

He turned back to the commander, and lowered his hands.

"You see how it is. It's better to die as heroes than walk the earth as cowards."

The commander looked at him a moment, and then at all the men, sweeping his gaze along their ranks as though to memorize the scene. He said nothing, but he bowed deeply from his saddle, then deftly nudged his pony into a trot back toward his ranks.

Radatan knew they did not have long to wait for the final charge. One more was all it would take. But he had done what he could for Shar. He gripped tight his spear, and waited.

13. Break It Like A Stick

Radatan and his men gathered close. The end was fast approaching.

"Today, we have earned the name of warrior," he told them. "Our enemy respects us. Our friends will honor us. Shar will thank us."

"Is there really an afterlife?" one of the soldiers asked.

"We're about to find out," Radatan answered. "This much is certain though. Whatever happens after death, no one can take away from us how we lived."

It was not much of an answer, but he was not much of a philosopher. Nevertheless, the men seemed to be pleased with what he had said, and they took hold of their spears, offered up a prayer to the heavens and waited.

The Nagraks did not move straight away. There seemed to be a discussion going on, and as far as Radatan could see it involved the leader he had spoken to and a group of sub-leaders. Then the meeting was over abruptly, and a lone man rode a little way toward them. He thrust a spear into the ground, a red tassel tied to its top. Then he returned to the rest of the riders.

A long moment the riders remained still, their horses motionless as well, and the whispering breeze hissed softly among the dried grasses. The sun lowered and its weak winter shafts, yellow and fading, slanted over the Fields of Rah.

Then with a sudden shout the Nagraks wheeled and rode, and the thunder of their ponies' hooves rumbled. That noise faded swiftly, for the riders headed away from the small group on the crest of the slope, and they did not look back.

Radatan could barely believe it. "I guess the afterlife will have to wait."

His men laughed and cheered. Some went down to their knees and wept.

"Why?" one of the men asked. "I don't understand."

Radatan thought he did. "Their leader is not just a Nagrak, but a Cheng warrior. He has beaten us, and honors us. The spirit of chivalry moved him, as once it moved our ancestors in the time of the Great Emperor."

They lit torches then against the coming dark, and worked deep into the night to build a mighty pyre for the dead out of such timber as could be gathered from their surroundings. This they did not just for their own fallen but for the Nagraks.

The night was old when they set the pyre alight, and the men exhausted. Yet they stood a moment in silence after Radatan remembered the dead, and then they cast themselves to the ground to sleep.

Only the scouts kept a guard around the camp. If the enemy wanted them dead, they would be. By grace they had been allowed to live, yet Radatan knew it was the grace of the commander. A different force would take a different course of action. He slept, hoping that no such force was in the vicinity.

He woke to broad daylight the next day. The pyre was still burning, for logs had gone into its making. Likely it would still be burning down to embers all day and all the night following.

The Fields of Rah were empty. The enemy would have hastened to Tashkar, and Shar also. If they were both there a battle would soon begin, but at least it was one where the Nagraks held no advantage of ground, and where the rest of Shar's army might spill out from the town to assist. It would be extremely difficult for the Nagrak commander to navigate those tactical difficulties. For Radatan, haste was needed though. Should Shar get inside, and the enemy be without, his way to rejoin her was blocked.

They began to march. The spear was still there in the distance that the enemy commander had stuck in the ground. Radatan headed to it first.

The shaft was wet with dew when he reached it and pulled it from the earth. There was no message attached to it by string, or pinned to the ground by the head. Yet lifting it and turning it in the light he saw strange writing marked upon it.

"What is this?" he asked.

Several men looked at it and shook their heads. They did not know. Then one came and looked at it closely.

"My grandmother was a Nagrak," he said softly. It was something he did not seem to want others to know. "She taught me some of their customs. This is a sign of honor in their tribe. Their chiefs often give inscribed spears to those who have performed brave deeds."

"What does it say?"

"I'm not fluent with their writing. They use an ancient script, but I think it says something like this. *The horse can run all day. The wolf all night. True warriors fight even when there is no hope. It is their nature.*"

Radatan liked it. There was no saying like that among the Two Ravens Clan. Perhaps there should be.

"Take the spear," Radatan told the man. "Strike it into the earth near the pyre. Let it serve as an honorable marker for those who rest there ever more."

The man hurried away and did so. Radatan waited for him to return, and then they marched again. Many of them carried wounds, so they could not go swiftly. They went as fast as possible though, and they did so in the knowledge that if they were in another battle they would not be so lucky again.

During the day they came upon the marks of passage of a great many ponies. This was not the trail of their enemy of yesterday, but joined it. Not long after, they found also the passage of a third army, this one on foot.

"See how the hoof marks tread over the boot marks?" Radatan asked a man marching beside him.

"Yes. The sacrifice of yesterday was not in vain. We diverted the enemy to us, and they missed Shar."

"They must have caught up by now, though."

Onward the column marched, Radatan striding at their head. And soon they entered the land of cultivated fields again, and the river was close by.

Not long after they saw Tashkar, and then were greeted by scouts of Shar's army.

"What news?" Radatan asked.

"Only this. Tashkar is still held by your forces, but it's under siege by Nagraks who passed us by and cut us off just before we reached the city. In turn, the Nagraks now direct half their force back toward Shar."

"Has there been battle yet?"

"Not yet. Nakatath was trying to talk to the Nagrak commander last I heard."

Radatan knew how that would go. The man was one of high honor. Yet he would not disobey his instructions, whatever Shar said. He would follow them, and that meant destroying her army, if he could. And capturing, or killing, her.

"There will be battle," he said.

He hurried forward, and more scouts were revealed as they passed. They were thick in the area, and spreading out. Shar would want to know if, large as it was, this was the only Nagrak force within striking range. If so, she

96

would have more time to try to negotiate, should she want it.

He thought it likely though that she would determine quickly what sort of enemy commander she was dealing with. She would like him, but there was no point in delay. She would strike soon.

They came up to the rear ranks of Shar's army, guided by scouts, and a way was opened for them through the host. They had reached the middle of the army when a commotion began. In doubt, they slowed down. Then Radatan saw Shar riding toward them, Huigar and Boldgrim to her sides.

Nakatath reached him. She was no great rider, and even he could see that. Yet she swung down from the saddle in one graceful movement, and, to his surprise, embraced him fiercely.

"I'm so happy to see you!" she cried.

Embarrassed, Radatan stepped back and looked at the ground.

"I'm happy to see you too, Shar Fei."

She looked at him seriously. "I know what you did. I know what your men did." She glanced behind him and pointed at the warriors who followed. "You are heroes! All of you! And so are those who sleep on the Fields of Rah."

The men in Shar's army all around went down on bended knee, and then surprising Radatan once more, so did Shar.

"We will remember," she said loudly. Then she spoke to Radatan directly again.

"I received word of events from your messengers. My own scouts reported the battle you fought, but I could not intervene. I was too far away, and I had to turn my footsteps to Tashkar. I still fear another Nagrak army. I must get inside the city swiftly."

"I know. I expected nothing else. You are constrained by destiny, Shar Fei. I understand. My men understand."

She looked at him, her gaze unreadable for a moment, but he almost thought he saw tears forming in her eyes, then she leapt back upon her horse.

"See that these brave men receive food and drink!" she commanded, once more indicating the remnant of warriors that had returned. "And you, Radatan, I'll need your advice. Up you get!" And she patted the rear of her saddle.

He looked up at her and gave a tired grin. "I think not, Shar Fei. I'm no rider. Put two of us a horse, and I'll likely just fall off."

Shar thought a moment, then she jumped down off the pony.

"Then *you* ride, and I shall walk. You're safer from falling that way. Probably."

She seemed bubbling over with sheer joy to see him, so he could not refuse. He clambered onto the pony and they set off through the army.

Shar walked at the front, but her bodyguards were close by. In truth, he was one of them again for he did not wish to leave her anymore. He had led an army, and done well enough, but he was more at ease protecting her. That was what he was good at.

As they walked Shar called out at times. "See the hunter from the Wahlum Hills? He and his men are heroes!"

He found it uncomfortable, but it seemed to please Shar, and many in the army called out to him by name. Truly, Shar had dissolved the barriers of tribe and clan. This was one army, just as she intended to make the whole Cheng people one nation.

They came to her command area where the chiefs and leaders were gathered, and he dismounted, grateful for the pony but happy to be on his own two feet again. A fire was lit, and food was being cooked. Yet with her own hands Shar fetched him a goblet of watered wine and bade him drink.

"Hail to the heroes who died on the Fields of Rah," he said, and emptied the goblet in one go.

"Hail them," the others repeated.

Shar replenished his goblet, but this time he merely sipped it.

"So, have you spoken to the enemy commander yet?" he asked.

"I have. He's a fine officer. I wish he was on my side, but he can't be convinced. Loyalty is admirable, but his is misplaced."

Radatan sighed. "So what will you do?"

"I'll break his army like a stick."

This was the other side to her. She could be kind and thoughtful. She was a true friend. She was funny and full of heart. But there was such determination in her that she could tell a forest to get out of her way, and the trees would bend to her will. So it seemed, anyway.

"He's good," Radatan said. "Don't underestimate him. And if you can, try to allow him an escape."

He told her of the final encounter they had in their battle, and the inscribed spear he had left. She did not seem surprised.

"I'll do what I can," she said. "We must break through though and enter Tashkar quickly. Who knows what other forces are on the way. You gave me the opportunity to get here swiftly at great cost. I'll not let that sacrifice be wasted."

Even as she spoke Radatan saw messengers arrive, and there were others coming too. They rode ponies, and they were coming from all areas of the army.

"We are ready," the first reported, and the others did likewise when they reached her.

"Good," she answered. There was a man nearby with a horn, and no doubt he would give the signal to advance, but she said nothing to him yet.

He read her thought. She was worried that shamans had joined the enemy.

14. I Am She

Shulu made her way to the bar. There were trestle tables left and right, some of them occupied. The scent of cooking was in the air, and a hint of smoke from the hearth.

It was warm inside. It was like entering someone's house rather than an inn. Or at least it felt that way despite all the tables.

Paintings adorned the walls. There were scenes from some of the pivotal moments in Cheng culture, although there was nothing of Chen Fei. She regretted that, but it could not be helped. To display a picture of the emperor was to mark oneself as a heretic and to draw the eye, and ill will, of shamans.

She reached the bar and pulled up a stool. There was no one else there but a young woman who tended it. She was stacking some glasses and Shulu waited.

Behind the bar was a door, and through that could be heard the hustle and bustle of a kitchen. Just like in any home, that also was the heart of an inn.

The young woman came over and smiled, wiping her hands down on a clean linen apron.

"What can I get you, dear?"

"A glass of beer, thank you."

The woman made to pour it from a keg with a spigot, and Shulu, making sure again no one was close, whispered to her.

"The *Dragon's Breath* is a strange name for an inn. It invites being burned down."

The young woman went deadly still except for a slight tremble in her hand that held the glass.

After a long moment, the woman answered. "The dragon is our ancient friend."

"So she is," Shulu said.

All the passwords had been given, and each knew the other for who they truly were.

The woman spoke with enormous reverence. "You are *she*?"

"I am she."

Despite her reverence, the woman maintained an outward appearance of nonchalance. Her urge had been to bow, but she hid that. She was good at her job as a spy, and she gave no sign that anything unusual was going on, lest it be noticed. Shulu appreciated that. It was no accident though. Over the years she had employed the best, and they trained the best, like this young woman, very well.

At that moment, a new person entered the inn. It was a woman, hooded against the cold outside. She was tall and haughty, and she took a seat in the corner of the room with barely a glance around her.

Shulu took her drink, and spoke softly. "See me when you get a chance." She left the bar and sat down at an empty table. It was far from any of the others. The conversation she was going to have must not be heard by anyone, and she could not stay at the bar as that might be suspicious. The young woman also had to go around and check if anyone wanted anything, especially the newcomer.

The beer was good. Shulu drank it, enjoying the slightly bitter taste. Despite it being cold outside, she liked to drink beer. Others would drink nahaz, which was more warming, but it would bring back too many memories for her.

The young woman went about her business, sharing a few jokes with some of the people who were obviously regulars, and then went to the newcomer's table.

Shulu studied the new woman carefully. She had come in not long after. Was it possible the woman had followed her here?

She did not think so. She had been careful. There was no indication she had been followed at all, and yet there was something suspicious going on. Maybe it was only her own anxiousness playing tricks on her. Maybe.

The innkeeper spoke loud enough to be heard even by Shulu, but the other woman answered in quiet tones. And even inside, she kept her hood up. Perhaps she was still cold from being outside. It meant nothing, but Shulu decided to complete her business here quickly.

The innkeeper fetched a drink of some sort for the woman. It was not beer. Possibly it was nahaz, given the small size of the goblet. That meant nothing in a Nagrak inn. Nahaz was almost the national drink. How quickly the woman drank it though might indicate if she were a Nagrak or not.

On returning to the bar, the innkeeper passed on an order of food to the kitchen out back. That was good. Shulu would be long gone before the new woman had any reason to be out on the street herself.

Shulu watched as carefully as she could, giving the impression of only glancing around the room now and then, but as far as she could see the woman had not sipped even once at her drink. It was strange.

With a gulp, Shulu finished her glass of beer, caught the eye of the innkeeper and raised her empty glass. The innkeeper filled another and brought it over, wiping down the table with a cloth.

"What can I do for you?" the young woman asked in a whisper as she worked.

Shulu leaned forward a little so the innkeeper's body hid her and no one could see if she was speaking.

"I'll be here at the same time tomorrow. Get word to the one known as the Tinker to meet me."

The woman gave no answer, and merely gave the table a final wipe and walked away. She was young, but she was good. Shulu decided to arrange an increase in her wage.

As fast as she could, without drawing attention to herself, Shulu drank the beer. The sooner she left here the better. No doubt it was just anxiety and many years of caution that gave her a sense of urgency, but she had long since learned to pay attention to her instincts.

She was nearly done when a large group of revelers entered. Cold air seeped into the inn, and the fire in the hearth guttered and flared. The new patrons were loud and a little drunk. They had started the evening elsewhere.

"No more of this when Shar arrives," one young woman said. "We'll be on rations then."

"I doubt it," another answered. This was a young man, and he seemed drunker than the others. "We're the best of the best, us Nagraks. We're too many for her, even if her army was three times the size. We'll send her to hell before she gets near the walls."

"Maybe," a third said. This was an older man. He looked like he knew how to handle himself, even if he wore no visible weapon. "No battle is easy, and numbers can be deceptive. To get this far, Shar must be a good general. Else she'd already be dead."

"That's not patriotic!" the drunk man slurred loudly.

The older man shook his head slightly. He wanted this conversation to go no further. The shamans had eyes and ears everywhere, and the wrong opinion could see a man in jail, or worse.

"You're right," he said. "She has no chance."

The young man looked at him surlily. He wanted to pick a fight, no doubt. Drinking brought out the worst in some people, but he had nowhere to go now that the other man agreed. He let it go and called out to the innkeeper. "Beer! We want beer!"

He was *definitely* one who should not drink. And it was just as well for him that the older man was reserved. Had the matter been pressed, Shulu had no doubt who would win a fight between them. The young man would be on the ground, bleeding from his nose before he even saw a punch coming.

Her work here was done, for tonight. She drank the last of her beer and left. The attitude of the revelers was probably the same as all the people throughout the city. Shar might or might not come. It made them nervous, but most doubted there was any real danger. Some had a better understanding of the possibilities though.

She left the inn and braced herself against the cold air outside. It would be her job now to change the attitude of the people. To make them fear. Even panic. That would give the shamans a problem to fix other than Shar. And with divided attentions they were more likely to make a mistake.

Panic was contagious, too. It was a sickness that spread. If the populace felt genuine fear, going so far as to start fleeing the city, then it would spread to the shamans too.

The Tinker was just the man she needed for this. The sword was usually the last option. Words, spread in the right way, could do more damage than armies. And he knew words. He was a tinker, which meant he was also a storyteller. He could shape the mood of the city. Most of all, he was a spy. One of her best.

There were less people on the street than before. It was growing colder quickly, and most had already gone to their homes or found a nice inn to eat their dinner.

Shulu hurried along, and pulled her hood close over her head and her cloak tight around her body. A wind had begun to blow, and her figure was so slight that she felt the air slice through her.

She bent her head forward and pushed on. Doubt still nagged at her. Was it a coincidence the woman had come into the bar so soon after her?

Jumping at shadows every step was no way to live. At the same time, she had lived a very long time despite the shamans trying to kill her for over a thousand years. She would be dead many times over if she ignored those little flutters of alarm that bubbled up to her consciousness. Call it instinct, or the wisdom of her magic, or blind chance. They had saved her in the past, even if they more often proved to be born of anxiety only.

To her right was an alley, and on a whim she turned into this. The wind died down instantly, being blocked by the taller buildings on either side of the narrow path. The shadows were deep, and there was a drift of snow underfoot that made walking a little harder. It was such a place that few would dare to tread at night, but she was Shulu Gan and she feared little in the world, least of all the sudden blade of a cutpurse in the dark.

She came to a place where there was some sort of balcony above. She could only see the dimmest of outlines, for the shadows hid it. Yet the snowfall was lighter under it, and there she stopped and pressed herself against the wall.

It was just a precaution. If someone came down this way after her she was certainly being followed though. To be on the safe side, she loosed a tendril of her magic, and she wove about herself a spell of concealment. It

106

was just a little magic that would help hide what the deep shadows did not.

And then she waited.

15. Watched

Shulu waited, and the wind wailed over the rooftops of the buildings that gave her shelter.

Her eyes were accustomed to the dark now, but mostly she concentrated on hearing anything out of place. It was difficult to detect any noise other than the wind though. In the distance, some loose gate rattled as air buffeted it. There were strains of music from far away, and perhaps even the sound of voices accompanying it in song. A dog barked, then went silent, and then barked again.

Whatever undercurrent of anxiety had gotten into her, Shulu dismissed it. She was alone, and the sooner she returned to her bed and got a little sleep the better. Even so, she would wait just a little longer.

Almost instantly she saw a shadow that seemed to move at the mouth of the alley where she had come from herself, and where there was more light from the street outside. Then it was gone.

All her senses straining now, Shulu waited. A knife slipped into her hand with barely a thought. A shaman that relied on magic alone was a fool. Cold steel had served her well in the past, but her magic was ready too. She felt it rise within her, but she kept it down. If she were followed by one who possessed magic, then anything more than the spell of concealment she used might be detected. It was ready though. Ready to tower up and destroy, for the chances of a second person coming down this alley by accident so soon after her were slim.

The dark figure came into view again. It hugged the opposite wall, and it slipped along in the deeper shadows quickly, and moved slowly where there was more light.

Whoever it was had little fear for themselves. A reveler would carry a lantern. The city watch would do so too, and there would be several of them. Whoever this was, they felt at home in the dark, and confident they were a match for anything they found there. Otherwise they would not have come this way.

That made Shulu even more wary. Who *was* this? A shaman? An acolyte of the shaman sent to spy on her?

She had to know. If the other possessed magic, and Shulu guessed they did, the person was a threat. With great care she let a sliver of the concealment spell unfold and slip through the night toward the figure. Only someone of great power would detect it. If that were so though, Shulu would know a moment earlier than her magic was understood, and she would use that moment to attack with all the power left to her. With that, and the element of surprise, she had a good chance of victory.

The figure paused. Perhaps they sensed someone else nearby. Or maybe it was natural caution. The magic touched it, and Shulu knew straightaway it was a woman. She possessed magic too, but her talent was raw, untrained and not especially strong.

Shulu withdrew her spell and remained still. This was the woman from the inn. Somehow, she had followed her, probably all the way from the shaman's mansion. It was a dangerous situation. Shulu could kill her, but who was she? Who sent her? Who would miss her if she did not return?

Some shamans kept female acolytes, and trained witch-women. It was possible. If so, Shulu knew she had to think twice about returning. To send someone after her like this meant the shaman must suspect her. And yet...

There was another possibility. It was not the witch-woman herself, with whom she had a feud going, but might it not be her daughter? The gift of magic often ran in families.

The figure was moving again, flitting more quickly now from shadow to shadow. Whoever it was sensed danger, even as Shulu had done herself, but it was easy to dismiss such a feeling as being nothing more than nerves.

The figure was level with her now, but lost in shadows on the other side of the alley.

Shulu waited. Patience belonged to the victor, and soon the figure was moving again and heading toward the end of the ally. No doubt she feared getting too far behind where she now thought Shulu must be.

In a few moments the figure was more visible again at the end of the ally, and then it was gone. Shulu waited. There was no hurry now. Strange as it seemed, this dark alley was the safest place in Nagrak City for her.

The question of who the woman was remained. It was the same person who had followed her into the inn, that was certain. No one knew she would leave the mansion though. They could not have been waiting without on the off chance that sooner or later they might see her. No. They lived in the shaman's mansion, and had kept an eye on her inside it. That would narrow down the possibilities a lot.

Shulu turned her mind to *The Dragon's Breath*. Was it compromised? She did not think so. She had not been there long, nor had she been seen having any significant discussions with anyone. It was not unusual to go to an inn, and it was not far from her place of employment. There was no suspicion there. To be on the safe side

110

though, she would not hurry back to the mansion. Let the woman who had followed her wonder where else she had gone.

Another few minutes passed, and Shulu ventured out of the alley. She retraced her steps and went back the way she had come. There were not many people on the street, and no sign of anyone else there who had been left to keep watch. So far as she could see.

She took the long way back to the mansion. She was being watched, but they had lost her. The longer she took to get back the more places she could have been that were not the *Dragon's Breath Inn*, and that would reduce any suspicion of it.

The wind came in gusts. Here, on the open Fields of Rah, there was nothing to stop it. The city had always been windy. She did not like it. Neither the wind nor the city.

Chen had not liked it here either. He made it his capital because these people were the ones who least liked him, and as the old saying went he preferred to keep his enemies close.

His enemies *were* close, and one closer than most. Olekhai. Even thinking about the Prime Minister made her blood hot with fury. It was always thus though, throughout history. The great were betrayed by their friends, by those whom they trusted.

There was a stall ahead, and it sold roasted chestnuts. She bought some and ate. It made her feel a little warmer, and a little better. She had good memories of cold winter evenings with Chen. They would share chestnuts and plan for a future, only some of which ever came to pass.

At length, she turned her footsteps toward the shaman's mansion. It was time to get some sleep and rest. Events were coming to a head now, and the final battles were starting to shape up. She needed sleep, and strength. And luck.

Her mind drifted out to Shar. She was close now. Closer than she had been in a very long time. She yearned to go to her and help, but Shar did not need that. She had The Fifty for magic. What she needed from Shulu was what was being done. Keeping a close eye on the shamans. Sowing seeds of doubt. Sending fear through Nagrak City. That would help Shar win this war.

If it could be won at all.

Her time was close. She felt it in her bones, and for a thousand years she had prepared the path of vengeance against the shamans. She would *not* allow herself to die before the culmination of those schemes. She would *not* be defeated.

Nor could she live if Shar were defeated. They would torture and kill her, eventually, if that came to pass.

Shulu breathed slowly to calm herself. She could not endure the pain of such loss again. It might happen though. Despite all her lore and determination. Despite her schemes based on shreds of prophecy and the hints of gods over a millennia. The enemy might win.

Better to die now than see that.

Yet Shar was a true descendant of Chen Fei. His genius was hers. His strength of will was hers. Most of all, his luck was hers.

At last she approached the shaman's mansion. It was late now, and the cold had grown intense. Few were about on the streets, and it was past time that she found her bed and slept.

The mansion looked quiet. It was well-lit at the front, and here and there a light shone in a window. There was always someone up in the mansion. Evil never rested.

She approached the front door, the only one that remained open this late. It was guarded, as she expected.

112

She knew the password though, and probably some of the guards, often nazram in training, would know her well anyway. It was she who tended their injuries, and she had won their respect.

There was a narrow strip of garden on either side of the path leading to the door. Shulu slowed, her senses alert.

Walking slowly, she let a tendril of her magic slip out before her. There was nothing at first, but then in the deep shadows she sensed someone in hiding. There was a familiarity to the person, and a sense of the magic she possessed. It was the same woman who had followed her to the inn and then the alley.

That the woman was following her was almost certain before, but now whatever slim doubt there had been was gone. She had lost her target, and failing to follow her had made her way back to this entrance to spy on her return.

Shulu was glad that she had delayed. And though the cold was bitter, at least she had been walking. This woman had waited, still and alone in the shadows of a bush all this time.

With the slightest of grins Shulu walked on. She was ready for an attack, but she did not think that likely. Not yet, and not here, at any rate.

She came to the guards and gave the password. It was instantly warmer inside, but not safer. Someone suspected her, and it was only a matter of time before an attack was made or she was caught spying.

No matter. She had always been ready for that, and now at least she knew one of her enemies beside the shaman. If not her face, at least by the sense of her magic. It might be the difference between life and death later on.

The corridors were dim, and she did not take her normal route back to her room. She must be unpredictable from now on. She must never be where she was expected. That would, of course, be difficult down in the training yard.

At least down there she would always be in plain view. That would mean nothing if the shaman went against her though.

It might not be the shaman who was having her watched, however. More and more she suspected the witch-woman had put one of her friends up to it, or recruited a daughter or granddaughter. She must ask around, subtly, if the witch-woman had such a relative in the mansion. It would be dangerous though, for the question might get back to the witch-woman and that would alert her.

Immediately on entering her room she knew that someone had been here. The bed had been searched, for the blanket was not in the exact position it had been left in that morning. So too the chair had been shifted. They were only minor changes, but their position had been memorized, and any deviation at all could only mean one thing.

It was not unexpected. It *was* disconcerting though. She was watched, and her time here was running out. Sooner or later, and possibly sooner, she would be discovered. Only those who were suspected were watched. And it did not matter who was doing the suspecting. Even if it were not the shaman, whoever it was would give him any evidence they found.

Carefully, she leaned the chair against the door so that if someone tried to open it they would find it difficult. At the very least, it would make sufficient noise to wake her up.

Against the window she wove a tendril of magic as a ward. It was barely there. Even the shaman, should he come into the room, might fail to detect it. Yet it would give her warning of someone coming in that way. That was unlikely given the height of her room, but her enemies were also the Ahat, and assassins like them, highly trained, had the skill and equipment to easily overcome such obstacles.

She slept then, but lightly.

16. Stirring the Pot

The wind died overnight, and the next day was warmer. However, out in the walled-in training yard at the rear of the shaman's mansion, the sun had not yet risen high enough to reach over the walls. There, it remained cold and a dusting of snow covered the ground.

It did not deter the warriors from training. Some sparred with wooden or metal blades. Others hand to hand. Another group were exercising, going through a myriad of ancient stretching and strengthening exercises.

One man practiced a sword form, and Shulu's gaze was mainly on him. He had skill. Like the best fighters, he was smooth and relaxed. He did not rely on strength, though his strikes were powerful. He relied on timing and the intricate shifting of his body weight.

He still had much to learn though. She had seen it all before, and her eye for skill was better than most of even the best warriors. She had been watching such things for so long that it was second nature to her. It did not matter that she was no good with a sword herself. She *saw*.

A knife was a different weapon though. She had some skill with that. It was not wise to rely on magic alone. Not that cold steel was void of magic itself. The forging of metals was a kind of sorcery, and a blade that was light yet strong, whose edge was hard to blunt, might mean the difference between life and death in a fight. That was why, of old, metalsmiths were revered. Even worshiped. They possessed the answer to mysteries that others did not.

Yet like all skills in the empire that was, in the shadowed remains of the greatness it once clothed itself in, the craft of metallurgy had gone backwards.

It was thus with all crafts. The shamans deliberately kept the people backward and uneducated, all the while saying how the advancement of the tribes was their priority.

The shamans were liars. They were corrupt to the core, and hypocrites. They did the things they falsely accused their enemies of doing, and they were skilled in their falsehoods. It was a lesson for any empire, at any time. The corrupt sought power, and those who proclaimed their righteousness were often the most void of morals.

If a society realized too late what was happening, and did not topple such rulers swiftly, it might be a thousand years before the chance to do so came again.

She looked around the training yard. There were many men there of varying ages. Most believed what they were told. A few understood the nature of power, and those who wielded it.

Her gaze fell on the shaman, who sat in discussion with some strange men at a bench at the side of the yard. He was looking at her, and she felt her instinctive hatred of him flare. She hid it though. Nevertheless, he frowned. Certainly too much had happened for him not to be suspicious of her.

Looking away, her glance fell to the witch-woman on the opposite side of the yard. She was mopping down a slate floor where the men often washed by the wall of the mansion. She too was looking at Shulu.

The shaman had appeared curious, or disturbed. It was different with the witch-woman. There was enmity there. Hard. Cold. Calculating. Her duties had been changed, and not for the better. There was reason

117

enough there to hate, but there was something else as well. Maybe just a conflict of personality.

That morning Shulu had fallen in step along a corridor with a young woman who helped clean the mansion. They were friendly with each other on a passing basis, and Shulu had broached the subject of the witch-woman with her, as subtly as she could, merely suggesting she had seen someone with a strong family resemblance. The cleaner did not know much about her, but did not think she had a relation in the mansion. Not that she knew of, anyway.

Shulu had let the matter drop as though it were just a passing idea. She could not risk asking anyone else though. It was too strange a question. The whole matter was annoying, but there was nothing she could do just at the moment except exercise extreme caution.

The day's work slipped by quickly with the normal amount of sprains and bruises. One man had been knocked unconscious by a blow to the head, but even that was not so unusual. Learning to be a warrior was a dangerous business.

At last the sun set and the training ceased for the day. A bell peeled, indicating dinner would soon be served in the dining hall.

Shulu made her way there, deep in thought. It would be best not to go to the *Dragon's Breath* tonight, despite arranging to see the Tinker there. Yet what she needed done could not wait. It was urgent, so the risk was worth it. She would be triply sure that she was not followed again tonight though.

She ate a little of the food that was served, and looked around as surreptitiously as she could. She spotted the witch-woman at another table. There was no sign though of the woman that had followed her to the inn last night. It was strange. And it was unsettling. Who *was* she?

118

Dinner ended and she went back to her room. There she waited for a good hour, trying to ensure that if her room were watched no one would be suspicious.

She guessed that after so much time anyone who had been watching would have left. They could not lurk in the corridor endlessly without arousing questions.

Moving quietly to the door so that no one could hear her, she jerked it open quickly and looked outside. There was no one there.

So far, so good. She moved quickly along the corridor, and then descended several sets of stairs. She was careful to choose a route that was not the direct way from her room to the main doorway at the front of the mansion. Probably it was the only one still open.

There was nothing unusual in the corridors, nor did she see anything out of place when she exited. She swept the gardens with her magic, and found nobody there.

That only made her more anxious. Better the enemy that could be found than the enemy who was hidden. There was nothing to do though but go on.

Just as she had in the mansion, she took an indirect route to the inn. It was not as cold as last night, and there was no wind. It was still more than cold enough to wear her hood up though, which she did. Only someone who worked with her closely in the mansion had a chance of recognizing her. There were people up and down every street that looked just as she did, all hurrying on their way.

At length she came near the inn. She stopped at a street stall, one of a great many through the city, that sold roasted chestnuts. She bought some and ate them nearby, keeping the cloth in which they had been wrapped. All the while she scrutinized the surrounds of the inn.

Here, too, nothing seemed out of place. Everything was as it should be. Of course, it was possible someone was watching from within one of the buildings nearby. If so, they would be invisible. But these buildings were mostly private residences. It seemed unlikely.

She pulled her hood back and tied the cloth as a headscarf in its place. At least she would look different from last night. Then she moved toward the inn.

Nothing seemed out of place, so she went inside. It was busier than yesterday, but she saw the Tinker at a table by himself straight away. She had never met him, but she knew his description. He studied her as she entered, and his eyes narrowed. He would not know what she looked like, but she was an old woman and that would immediately mark her.

He ignored her after that, and she went to the bar for a drink. The same woman was serving, and she poured a beer without comment and gave no indication they had ever met or spoken before. That was just as it should be.

Shulu looked around the room. The woman who had followed her last night was not here. That was good, but it did not mean another had not been sent to watch.

She made a show of choosing a place to sit, and finally sat at the same table as the Tinker.

He eyed her cautiously. "A strange name for an inn," he said. "It almost invites the place being burned down."

"The dragon is our ancient friend," she replied, giving the counter sign.

There was a pause while they both sipped at their beers, and looked around carefully to see that no one was watching them.

"What can I do for you?" he asked softly.

The faster she did this the better. There seemed to be no one here watching them, least of all the woman from last night, but the more time they spent together the greater the danger for both. And the inn.

"You have heard that Shar Fei is not far away? With an army?"

"I have."

"Take that information. Foment a rumor. Spread it across the city until it blazes like a grassfire on the Fields of Rah. She marches on Nagrak City, a massive army at her command, and she will level it to the ground."

He looked at her calmly. "Shar is not heading here then?"

Shulu had not met the man before, but she knew much about him. He was shrewd. He had an intellect that could grasp the hidden easily, and experience that taught him to doubt what others readily believed. She could not treat him like a fool. Nor did she want to reveal too much, in case he were captured and interrogated.

"Maybe. And maybe not. No doubt you'll form your own theory, but you'll understand why it's best I say nothing."

He nodded curtly. "I understand. But this rumor, it already runs rampant."

"True. That gives you a lot to work with. I want you to stir the pot though. Intensify it manyfold. The populace thinks they're protected. But are they? Is the Nagrak army a match for Shar, who has already swept all before her? Will she not do the same here, and raze to the ground the city where her forefather and all her ancient family were assassinated? Will she not unleash a torrent of blood to run through the streets? Probably there is such a prophecy…"

The Tinker understood. He was, in fact, a tinker by trade. He dressed like one, and his face was browned by the sun and his skin wrinkled. He moved around the city and the hinterland, mending things and selling small items. He moved in the lowest circles, and in shops and in the mansions of the rich. But for all that he appeared, he was also one of the smartest people in all the Cheng Empire. He was wealthy, having investments throughout Nagrak City under his real name, and who, in different guise, moved among the highest ranks of society. He was two men in one, but this was the real one. This was the one who hated the shamans.

"I understand what you want. It will be done, and fast. Whatever Shar does, she is supposed to be fairly close already. The rumor will swiftly die if she moves away from us though."

There was nothing else to say. Not of importance. They both sipped their drinks and talked more loudly of inconsequential things, such as the warmer turn in the weather.

The innkeeper was busy, and she ignored them. There was nothing going on that would give anyone cause for suspicion, and no indication that anyone here was doing anything other than enjoying a drink and a good meal. Nevertheless, Shulu finished her drink quickly.

"Good luck," she said quietly to the Tinker, and stood to leave.

"Good luck," he replied. He still had a little left to drink and he would wait a long interval before he left so as to make sure no one thought they were associated.

Shulu went to leave. She cast her gaze subtly around the room to see if anyone was watching her, but everyone seemed intent on their conversations with friends. Or they were eating or drinking. There was nothing that aroused her suspicion. Even so, something was not quite right. She just did not know what it was.

Moving to the door she went outside. There she paused a moment, allowing her eyes to adjust to the darker environment.

There were a few passersby, but no one looked at her, or paid her any attention at all. She stepped onto the street and began walking. Even as she did so her skin tightened with goosebumps, and the hair on the back of her neck prickled.

17. A Daughter of the Night

Shulu stood where she was. No one seemed to notice anything out of place around her, or to be alarmed in any way. Yet she felt the weight of dread. Something dangerous was nearby. Something of which to be very afraid.

She saw nothing though. Not until the woman from last night stepped out from behind a group of pedestrians and strode toward her. She was unmasked now, and made no effort to hide her enmity. Or her power. Yet only Shulu could see it.

"Begone!" Shulu's voice cracked out like a whip. She did not speak to the woman, but to the pedestrians. They did not know their danger, and that in moments death would fly through the street and haunt it. For the woman had come to do battle. Her intent was clear, and she cared nothing that this was a public place.

The pedestrians looked on, puzzled for a moment, thinking merely that someone crazed walked among them, but some saw the other woman, and the eldritch light that sprang up about her.

"Sorcery!" some screamed, and ran. And even those who had seen nothing felt the wave of panic and ran with the others.

Suddenly the street was empty, and only Shulu stood there, still as a statue, the young woman facing her, hands balled into fist through which the light of magic flared like a part-shuttered lamp.

They studied each other in silence, each weighing the other up. A fight to the death was coming, and now the crowd and the street and the city were all forgotten. There was only the two of them in all the world, trying to read the soul of the other, and what power and courage they had.

"Who *are* you?" the woman asked.

It was a tactic to stall for time. Evidently, the woman had expected fear, and was surprised that Shulu had shown none. That bespoke of confidence and power. Much, much more than Shulu had thought last evening. This woman had such power that she could mask it and conceal her true nature.

"I know who *I* am," Shulu answered. "Who are *you*?"

It was a mistake. Asking a question showed her own doubts.

"Let us find the answer to both our questions then," the woman said. Power rose up through her as though in a wave from the earth, and when she snapped out her arms wicked fire shot from them.

Shulu was ready. A shield of white burgeoned before her, thin as mist but solid as a mountain to magic. Or so she thought. The attack hit it, and sent her staggering backward. The white light flickered, nearly fading, and then strengthened again. Shulu had rarely felt such power. Whoever this was, it was no daughter of the witch-woman as she had thought. Nor an acolyte to the shaman. This woman's power was greater than his.

The woman laughed. "You are weak and old. This will be delightful."

There was a hint of madness there. The woman's eyes were feral, like a wild animal that was diseased. News of their fighting would spread through the city rapidly, and the shamans would sense it and come. The forces unleashed were great, and they could not be hidden. That would be a terrible thing for Shulu, and so she must win this fight swiftly and escape.

125

If she could.

The woman watched her, eyes alight now with a fire of their own, and she circled Shulu like a cat stalking a mouse.

With a sudden leap forward the woman came at her, both arms flinging fire in turns. Shulu, too old to dodge properly, used her shield as a defense, but each blow sent her staggering backward. She veered to the side, but the woman pursued her relentlessly, fire lighting up the street and casting massive shadows against the buildings.

The street was empty now, except for them, but from far away came screams and cries of fear.

Shulu staggered back again, nearly forced to her knees by the power unleashed. The magic felt strange to her too. It was not shaman magic such as her own. Whoever this was she was not trained by her enemies or related to the witch-woman.

She let her shield waver, and dropped to one knee. The woman came in for the kill, but Shulu sent a whip of fire under her shield. It leaped out, lashing the woman's legs and pulling her to the ground.

Shulu released her shield. She did not have the strength to defend and attack properly at the same time. She ran forward and cast a spear of fire at her attacker.

The woman dodged, coming to her feet and leaping away. There was a boom as though of rumbling thunder, and the flagstones of the street cracked and ruptured at Shulu's blast, exposing the soil below them. Out of the crevice tongues of flame darted.

Shulu leaped over it, and conserving her strength relied on steel. A blade flew from her hand, and then another while the first was still in flight.

The woman leaned out of the way of the first, the spinning blade driving past her face to clatter on the

126

street behind, but the second took her in the shoulder. She screamed, her head back like an animal.

Shulu understood then. This was not a creature of Alithoras. At least not now. This was a summoning from the ancient world. Even as the tagayah had been summoned, so too this. It was what the old legends called a fury.

It made sense to her now. A fury. A daughter of the night, as they were called in legend. A creature of viciousness, stealth and power. To bring her forth would have required blood magic. That was a specialty of some witch-women. It did not require great power, but dark lore. The sort employed in hidden caves up in the lonely hills where outlawed witches gathered for dark rites.

The fury hissed and leaped at her. The guise that had veiled her began to fail, and her face was now feline, her ears growing back and her teeth pointed as they tore at Shulu's neck.

Drawing magic to her hands Shulu grabbed hold of the creature and flung it away. It landed on four feet now, part human and part animal.

Shulu felt sick. She was too old for this, and unless she killed this thing and fled soon she would be surrounded by shamans as well. Yet she had defeated the tagayah, and that was more dangerous.

She stood tall. Some of the pride and power of her youth came to her. With a flourish of her hand she summoned a writhing mass of flame and flung it at the fury.

The creature leaped away, quick as thought. Yet the magic caught it a glancing blow and sent it cartwheeling. Shulu wasted no time, striding in and throwing magic at it with one hand and then the other, rending the flagstones and sending sheets of flame running like water across the street.

Again the creature leaped at her. With one fiery hand Shulu held it at bay, yet she was knocked to the ground. With the other hand she sought her last knife from the holding loop within her cloak. The breath of the beast was upon her face, and her strength, physical and magical, began to ebb.

The blade struck home. Deep it penetrated, and the creature screamed and rolled away, blood dripping from the wound and hatred in its eyes. And for the first time, fear.

But a fury was a thing of wild magic, hatred and chaos all rolled into one. It came at Shulu again.

Shulu dared not cast her last knife. She might need it if her magic failed her. She lifted high her other hand, prepared to send another blast of magic, but she saw a child run out from a building behind the fury. She hesitated, unable to send the killing magic.

The beast crashed into her, jaws snapping from a face that was now part human and part feline. They both sprawled over the pitted street, and came up to face each other again.

Of the child, there was no sign. The knife that had been in her hand now lay on the street between them, knocked out of her grip when they fell. The creature charged at her again.

In desperation, Shulu strode forward to meet it. She *must* kill it soon. Holding up her two hands she pulsed a wall of flame outward. The fury smashed into it, and then through it, hands, now tipped with claws, flashing through the air.

Shulu dropped low. The beast passed over her head. Quickly Shulu retrieved the fallen blade, and in one motion turned and thrust.

The fury had leaped again. Its clothes were on fire, and the stench of burning flesh filled the air. Again they toppled to the street, and this time the weight of the creature was fully upon Shulu.

The creature bit at her neck. Shulu stabbed with the blade. Again and again it struck home, and she felt warm blood flow over her.

With a burst of magic and the last of her strength, Shulu threw the fury from her and staggered to her feet. The creature was all beast now, tattered clothes hanging about it and its fur matted with blood. It jumped at her again, but slipped on its own entrails that cascaded out of a gaping wound. Shulu gritted her teeth and summoned magic.

It did not come. She was tired and old. For the first time in her life her power had deserted her, yet she strove to bring it to bear and a moment later flamed leaped at her fingertips.

She directed it at the creature, and with a final hiss it died, claws scrambling over the paving stones.

Shulu staggered away. She headed for the alley that she had used last night. Once inside it, she paused to catch her breath. How long before a shaman arrived? It could be any moment. If she were caught she was too weak to fight again.

There was nothing she could do though. She needed a moment's rest, and she was at least away from the immediate scene of battle. Her cloak was ripped in places, and covered with blood. It was not hers, but it would draw attention to her. She cast it aside. Then she made to move away, but paused.

She had been seen in that cloak. There was nothing special about it, but should it be found it might help identify her. It was difficult, but she summoned enough magic to burn it, and then she left.

At the end of the alley she paused. There was no one there. The street was empty. All doors were closed, and where there were windows with shutters, they were closed too. The noise of the fight and the panic had spread this far, but soon she hoped she could meld into a group of people. Until she had that cover she stood out far too much.

Moving quickly through the street she came to another alley. Better to be out of potential sight and risk the dangers of such a dark place where theft and murders were common. In the middle of it, she paused. From the street ahead came the sound of booted feet running. Many of them. It must be a platoon of the city watch. She let out a breath of relief as they passed without turning into the alley themselves.

At the exit she paused in the shadows. There was no one, but she heard calls in the streets around her and horns blowing. It was more of the watch.

She darted out, as quickly as her tottery legs would take her. Then she found another alley and a different street. Here there were pedestrians. They seemed unsettled, but they were far enough away that they had not seen the fight or known what had happened.

Shulu fell into a steady pace on the street, walking behind a group of young men. They seemed drunk and must have just left an inn, but the unsettled clamor on the streets around them had sobered them up. They walked quickly and with intent, probably heading for their homes.

A few minutes later and Shulu was well away. There were people everywhere now, and things seemed almost normal. Walking toward her was an older woman by herself. Likely she was close to home, for women rarely traveled far from home at night.

"Excuse me," Shulu said to her. "My daughter is ill and I've forgotten my cloak. Can I buy yours?"

The woman looked at her strangely, as well she might, then shook her head.

"I need it myself." She went to walk on quickly, but Shulu stood in her way.

"Please. She's on the other side of the city. And I'm in a hurry." Even as she spoke she showed a gold coin in her hand. It was more than the woman would earn in a month, and she stared at it.

"What's this really about?"

"I just need the cloak. And you want the money. Does anything else matter?"

The woman did not hesitate long. After a searching gaze, she took off the cloak and gave it to Shulu, who passed her the gold coin.

Without another word, Shulu hastened ahead. It would have been better not to have done this. It was a contact point where her description could be found. But she needed that cloak to avoid looking suspicious entering the mansion. That would be even worse. Besides, the woman could probably not give a good description, and the headcloth would confuse things too.

Pulling up the hood, she removed the headcloth and cast it into a bin. She felt better now, and her strength was returning. The fight had been unexpected and vicious, and only by luck had she avoided being killed or discovered. By now, there must be a dozed shamans at the site where the fight had taken place.

The *Dragon's Breath Inn* was in danger. They might be questioned, but Shulu did not think any connection could be made. The fury was not summoned by the shamans, but the witch-woman. And having discovered Shulu going back there for the second night, she had been killed before she could report it.

Coming close to the mansion she studied it. There were no signs of unusual activity. She went ahead, and made a point of talking to the guards at the front entrance and joking with them. If they were asked later about her, they would say she appeared perfectly at ease and not like someone who had been in a death fight.

She came to her room, and closed the door and positioned the chair under the knob as usual. Her blood began to boil with anger. The witch-woman had summoned the fury. It was vengeance magic, dark and forbidden. It required the blood sacrifice of a human.

That made the witch-woman a deadly enemy, and Shulu now had no qualms about killing her. If she could. To kill her though was to have the finger of suspicion pointed directly against her because their enmity was well known. And she could not survive any further scrutiny.

If she did not act though, what might the witch-woman try next?

18. Such is Leadership

Kubodin felt sick. He sat before the hearth, a log burning briskly, the red embers of the one before underneath it as a bed.

One of his own aides had betrayed him. It was unthinkable, but the lure of money, or the cult of the shamans, was a strong force. Both drove people to acts that could not be justified. The one by temptation and the other by fanaticism.

He tried to think of something else, but could not. The man was being questioned now, and that questioning would be brutal. The Cheng tribes did not treat traitors kindly, and men had died because of his treachery.

Kubodin cast his mind back. On a time, in his youth, he had been tortured and still bore the scars. Asana had saved him, but there would be no Asana for this man. To save himself, he must speak. If he were a fanatic though, he might not.

Despite his own history, Kubodin had given the order, and this man might be subjected to the unspeakable. He wanted to vomit, and yet if he did not give the order, others would die. Perhaps hundreds or even thousands. Who could say how deep the treason ran, or even if it went to a chief?

Kubodin did not believe it would, but he could not know for sure. Without Shar here, there were those who might waver.

So he sat before the fire, cold at heart and waited. And waited some more, until in the late stretches of the night Argash, who was in charge of the questioning came to him.

The other chief looked bleak. But he was a Fen Wolf, and that tribe often did. Even Shar seemed stern at those times of greatest triumph, but he had learned that her face rarely spoke of what she was feeling.

"What did you learn?"

"Precious little," the other chief answered.

Kubodin grunted. He was not happy, but he had expected as much.

"He spoke a lot," Argash went on, "but he had no real information. They did it for money. There are others in the fortress, but they had a different leader. The groups were kept apart so that if one were discovered they could not identify the other. He did not think the other group was large though."

That was all to be expected. None of it was anything he had not considered, but at least it was confirmation.

"You believed him?"

"We think he was telling the truth. The story never changed, no matter what."

No matter what. Those were words that said little but meant much.

"And what happened after that?"

"We gave him the choice of hanging, poison or a knife to slit his wrists."

That had been discussed earlier. Traitors must be executed to discourage others from following the same path. Some had suggested he must be hanged, but the man had given himself up and cooperated. He deserved to choose himself how to die, and Kubodin had ensured he had that small grace.

"He took the poison?"

Argash nodded.

It was the best way for a warrior. Hanging was for criminals. A cold blade for the suicidal. But poisoning for the warrior sick at heart for what he had done.

Kubodin shook off the lethargy that was overtaking him. It was a grim business, and he was still recovering from his wounds.

"Come morning," he said, "let the truth be known. Spread it far and wide. A small group of traitors, plotting against us, was discovered and killed. If there are any more, they too will be found."

Argash left him then, and Kubodin stared into the flames. The new log had caught and blazed, but now it too was dying in turn.

"You should sleep."

It was Ravengrim who spoke. Somehow the man always seemed able to slip up to him undetected. It was annoying, but he was a shaman. Perhaps he used magic, in which case it would not be so bad.

"I know. I'm tired, but I don't feel like it. Too much has happened, and more is to come."

The shaman pulled up a chair and warmed his hands before the fire.

"Talk to me then. Share your burden."

At least he was wise enough not to try to force a patient to bed. The only thing worse than not sleeping was lying in bed and trying to but failing.

Kubodin sighed. "It's not so complicated. Shar left me in charge, but leadership isn't easy. Every soul in this fortress is my responsibility. By my wit, they live or die. That's a heavy weight for a man to carry."

The shaman did not answer at once. He stared a long while into the fire, then he roused.

"Death calls to every one of us. My time is close. The time of the Fifty is close. We will not survive this war. It is something we long have guessed, but now we know.

135

From our ashes something new will rise. But you? You bear much responsibility. And you bear it well. You did not ask for it. Rather it was thrust upon you. That is why you feel it keenly, and why you do well. Perhaps you will survive this, and your army with you. For what it is worth, I think you will."

It was unnerving to hear the shaman speak so. Almost he asked him questions about what he thought his future was, and the rest of the Fifty. He was a shaman though, and they rarely spoke much that was plain, and it was clear from his face that he would say no more on that subject.

"Is the enemy doing anything new?"

The old man looked into the fire, and his gaze was far away.

"They sit and wait. The cold is biting them now. Firewood is in short supply. Sickness runs through them, both mental and physical. The shamans are in disarray after what has happened, and I think we are safe for a time. The enemy shamans will not rest though. You can be sure of that."

Eventually Kubodin slept, yet he was still up early next morning and made a point to go to the battlements. His wounds still troubled him, but he was healing fast. And it was better to be here than in the barracks. Here, just by being seen, he could do some good.

It had snowed a little overnight, and the open spaces below the fortress were dusted with snow. It almost looked pretty, but the stench of rotting corpses was in the air, if faint. Come summer the smell would be worse.

He was surprised the enemy had not arranged parley to collect their dead. It did a live soldier rushing the walls no good to see what his fate would be, but perhaps the shamans thought they could just drive the men forward anyway.

136

Or it might be an indication that they had given up on fighting. That was a worrying thought. If so, what did they have planned instead?

Snow began to fall again, and Kubodin liked it. The soldiers down below were suffering. For them, he felt a deep well of pity in his heart. Pity had little place in the tactics of war though. The weather was a weapon, and at the moment it was his to use. He would not have put it aside even if he could.

A soldier's state of mind was also a weapon, and much of any battle was won or lost before a blade was drawn. He glanced at one of his aides, wondering if he could trust the man. No good would come of letting that anxiety overwhelm him though. He had been betrayed, but that did not mean all men were traitors.

"Send word," he told the aide, "to the generals. Let them find as many braziers as they can, and start fires on the battlements for our soldiers to warm themselves."

The man hurried away. Kubodin looked out at the Nagrak horde again. They were suffering, and here he was rubbing salt into the wound. It could be a mistake. It might stoke their hatred for Shar's army. More likely though it would fuel resentment at the shamans who led them. If things got bad enough, and what could be worse than seeing an enemy in comfort while you yourself suffered, might not a revolt start?

He hoped so. The shamans had tried to win the battle by devious means. Two could attempt that though. He would talk to the generals later and see if they had any suggestions. There might be other ways to fight this battle of the mind. Perhaps they could even consider sending spies into the enemy camp. If they were successful, they could start spreading rumors designed to undermine the shamans. That would help any revolt that was already brewing.

So much for his plans. He knew and understood what he was doing. What of the shamans though? What plans were they concocting, or had already set in motion?

19. Age of the Archer

The midnight air was cold, but it was also clean and fresh. Olekhai liked it. The world was a quiet place at this time of night, and the darkness opened up ways to see not grasped by lesser men.

In the pagoda it was not quite silent. Timbers creaked in the growing cold. The slate roof was slick with frost, but where he sat on a special observatory on the very peak, ringed around with rails and floored by oiled timber, he had room to stand, walk, sit or lie and observe the heavens in safety. He could not fall. Not that falling would kill him anyway.

He had tried falling before. It brought long periods of pain, but never death.

Yet here, he could almost forget his curse. He was one with the cosmos. The consciousness of the universe itself, looking back at its own physical form.

That was something to rejoice in. Of all the empires of Alithoras, over all the ages, perhaps none had grasped the arts of star-watching as had those people who would become the Cheng.

The line of their wisdom was unbroken to him. He had learned from his master, who had learned from his back into the days of darkness. The Cheng had learned it from the Letharn, who in turn had learned it from their predecessors whom history had forgotten.

His knowledge was nearly as old as humankind, but was yet as a child learning to crawl compared to the universe, old beyond measure, that had spawned self-awareness.

He gazed up, and the wonder of the stars dizzied him. Almost it seemed he floated amid them, for the pagoda was high and no earthly lights from nearby drowned the heavenly glory.

The cycle of the stars was almost complete. Twenty five thousand and nine hundred years ago, the Age of the Archer had begun. Now a new age was dawning, and the twelfth constellation in turn ruled the heavens.

As it is above, so it will be below. Those were the words of his master, and he believed them. It was a time of change and destiny. Stories from all over the continent were reaching his ears. Battles. Wars. Kings. The rise of the Dark and the rise of the Light.

It meant nothing to him. The earth could spin its predetermined course through the heavens, or veer into chaos and oblivion. The gods could rule. Or fall. He cared nothing for any of it. He sought only release from the curse.

But in a time of change where destinies ebbed and flowed, and in an epoch where the Light became Dark and the Dark Light, all things were possible for him too. If he rode the currents of destiny he could free himself of the terrible curse placed upon him, and gain vengeance on Shulu and the upstart offspring of the dead emperor.

He lay back and gazed at the stars. He knew so many of them by name. He knew all the constellations and their properties. He understood the invisible light from them that pulled on the strings of fate, that guided the deeds of humanity. They seldom knew what influenced them, and how their plans succeeded and failed according to the invisible nudges of the universe. *He* knew though. He knew and understood.

The shamans had some knowledge. But they dabbled in the mystical numbers of thirty six and one hundred and eight. Foolishness. Ignorance. That was just a part of the grand cycle. It was just a part of the great conflux happening now. Perhaps he alone in all Alithoras still remembered and understood the true lore.

He read the book of the heavens, and he liked what he learned. There came a knock on the trapdoor in the floor that disturbed his tranquility though.

"Come!" he said impatiently.

The door lifted up, and a man clambered onto the platform. Olekhai's annoyance eased away. This man was one of his best spies. An assassin too, but a better spy. He had proved invaluable over his lifetime, but he was old now.

The man bowed with the proper reverence, even if age had rendered his legs weak and he could not lower himself to the expected degree.

"Speak, Nassa."

The man straightened, careful not to look Olekhai in the face. The pale starlight did not hide the ragged scar that crossed Nassa's cheek and nose, a relic from an assassination in his youth. Sometimes shamans fought back with steel.

"The search for Shulu continues, Great One."

"Is that all? Does that mean she is not found yet? How can that be so with all the men at your command?"

Nassa did not show a trace of fear. Others would be sweating by now, and this was one of the reasons to like him. He was sure of his abilities, and he knew he would be hard to replace.

"Shulu Gan, as ever, is elusive. No one can hide forever though, even in a city. There are over twenty possible sightings. Most of these will be error, but she may be one of them. I have a man who saw her once investigating each. Including one that involves a servant in a shaman's household."

141

Olekhai frowned. "Be sure to have your man investigate that household closely. It would be Shulu's sense of humor to hide in such a place."

"I will, Great One."

When Nassa had left, Olekhai reclined again and immersed himself in the ocean of the stars. Of late, there was a new one.

He found it now and studied it. It was not normal. It followed none of the rules, and traced no ordained path as the others. These recalcitrant stars the ancients called comets had long been known to those who read the book of heaven, and their meaning was clear.

Change. Cataclysm. A time of upheaval where the oceans drank the land, mountains toppled and islands rose from the churning sea. Kings died. Emperors rose. Nations bled their youth into the dust in fruitless war, and chaos rode supreme over the land.

He would ride the wave. Who better than he who had lived so long, who understood so much? He was not a shaman but a scholar. The shamans might perish, and he cared nothing for them. The tribes might disintegrate into family clans that lived in caves, or unite into a nation. He cared nothing for any of it.

But for Shar, he would move the earth. To control her, to use her to break the curse, and then break her in turn. That was what he wanted. That was what he had worked toward for years beyond count. Only *he* had truly believed the rumor that one of Chen's line had survived, and he had prepared for the day when Shulu would bring the scion forth to challenge the shamans.

The time was now. At long last the curse would be lifted, and if the earth was destroyed in the process, what was it to him?

He gazed at the stars and became one with them. His mind floated in the darkness, and he knew peace as he seldom did.

Even so, something disturbed him. Comets were not only a sign for change, but a harbinger of demonic force.

20. A Shadow of Uncertainty

Shar had divided her force into three, and they began to march, spreading out. She, with many of her leaders, were in the middle group.

Radatan glanced at her. "Why are we dividing up?"

"No reason," she answered, allowing the faintest of smiles to play on her lips.

He frowned. "Then why do it?"

"To make the enemy commander ask himself the same question as you just did. Why? Not for any other reason. But while he's trying to figure one out, he's thinking less about more important matters."

Radatan grasped her intent then, and said nothing. He was a quick learner. Deceive and misdirect were the great strategies of war. Whatever you wanted most, you must appear to want least. What you wanted least, you must appear to grasp at with eagerness. It was the game of war. It was the game of life and death.

She did not doubt the enemy commander was prepared for her though. Radatan had admired him, so he was good. He would soon discern that the way she marched meant nothing, but it would take longer for his captains to realize that or to receive communication from him.

Tashkar was close now. The enemy that barred the way of her entering was closer still. Would they fight in such a situation? They knew that at any time the force Radatan had left in the city might come out and attack. If so, they would be battling on two fronts.

No commander would expose his army to that, if he could help it. Likewise, he would be loath to move away and allow Shar to obtain her goal. For try to deceive as she might, there was no disguising that she intended to enter the safety of the city.

She felt sympathy for the enemy commander. He was in an excruciatingly difficult dilemma. How he reacted would say much about what was important to him. The lives of the men under his charge, or satisfying the shamans who held, in turn, the power of life and death over him.

Certainly the shamans would not care what losses were inflicted on this army. Massive as it was, the Nagrak tribe was so large they could muster another. Yet even they must admit that needlessly throwing away the lives of soldiers would work against them. A defeat like that would sink morale like a ship without a hull.

The three prongs of her attack moved forward. She had not been able to communicate with her forces within the city, yet they were there. She knew it, and the enemy knew it.

The enemy did not move. It seemed it would come to battle, and despite Shar's superior position, thanks to the efforts of Radatan, the outcome was not certain. She *should* win. She *hoped* to win. Victory was not guaranteed though.

Dusk settled over the land with a great stillness. It was cold, and a faint breeze rustled through the dead grasses and over the bare earth of the cultivated river plain nearby.

Shar was about to draw her swords. The sight of the fabled blades always gave her army heart, and they knew she fought with them. Where they marched, she marched. Where they held the line against the trampling onslaught of cavalry, she held the line. Where they risked their lives with courage, so too did she. It could not be otherwise for one who desired to raise a rebellion. Leaders must lead.

Even as her hands touched the hilts though, the enemy, by some unseen command, began to move. As one the horses turned, and they trotted briskly.

Like a swift-floating cloud in the sky the enemy passed on and left the way clear. Dusk was falling, and everything seemed peaceful. Only the threat of great violence averted hung in the air. And a sense of unease.

"The way is clear," Radatan said.

"So it is. But why?"

"You know as well as I. The enemy is smart. Better to face the dismay of the shamans than to destroy his army. He would not have won, and he knew it."

Such had been her own reasoning. And it was true, so far as it went. The outcome was not certain though. He might have won.

"I begin to wonder if there was not another reason?"

Radatan shook his head. "You worry too much."

"I do. But it's kept me alive for a long time. I'll not stop now."

"What do you worry about with this move of the enemy then? It seems to me that he's given you exactly what you wish. Entry into the safety of Tashkar."

Shar signaled the army onward. Come what may, they would sleep under a roof tonight.

"If the enemy allows entry into the city, it might be because he feared battle. I wouldn't blame him. But what if he knows the city isn't as safe as we hope?"

Radatan looked down into the ravine they were approaching.

"I've been down there," he said, pointing, "and up the other side. I tried to figure out how the place could be taken by force. I would have done it, but it would

146

have been a terrible battle, and the losses great. Now that you hold it, and by far, far greater numbers, it's nearly impregnable."

"All the more reason your enemy friend should have tried to stop me, yes?"

The old hunter turned that over in his mind a bit. "I take your point."

They descended the narrow path, and Shar ordered a defensive line of spearmen set at the rear. She did not trust that this was not a trap designed to allow an attack while her army was in a vulnerable position. This it would soon be in when the fore part began to enter Tashkar but the rear was isolated, waiting.

No attack came though. By nightfall, most of the army was inside and being quartered in barracks. These were underground, and it seemed the stories were true. This was a city of caves, and there seemed no end to them.

Shar contemplated the actions of the enemy commander. Was he sympathetic to her cause? That was possible. If so, why not join her? That did not seem to explain anything. Did he spare his men battle when the outcome was uncertain? That seemed more likely. It was standard training for a commander to avoid conflict when the outcome was not palpably in his favor. In this case, though, he would be giving her a great advantage, and he would have to justify that to shamans who did not have his own military training and merely wanted victories.

Or, and she began to think this likely, a massive enemy force was close by, and between the two of them she would be trapped in here, unable to act. If so, the numbers of the Nagraks were even greater than Shulu had told her.

147

There was another possibility, and she leaned toward this too. There were a group of shamans close by. And the enemy commander knew they intended to use sorcery to defeat her. At the moment, she only had her swords and Boldgrim as a defense against that.

The uncertainty of the situation annoyed her. She had thought her coming here was a great tactical move, but had the enemy anticipated her and led her into a trap?

She put those thoughts aside. They must wait for another time. Now, she must make a good impression with the elders of this city, and a meeting had been arranged with them.

The elders greeted her in a banquet room where refreshments were provided. Of the food and drink, she was wary. There was no easier way to end the rebellion than to kill her, and she did not know nor yet trust these people.

Holding a glass of wine, but not drinking from it, she spoke in friendly fashion with the elders.

"Radatan has informed me of all the arrangements," she said. "You'll have the gold within the hour. I keep my word, and you will find that I'm a good ally."

This seemed to please them, and the conversation turned to other matters.

"Are you really the descendant of Chen Fei?" one of the elders asked. She did not think he was being rude, but merely curious.

With her violet eyes staring deep into his own, she replied.

"I am. Who else but a descendant can wield these swords. And who else could unite the tribes as I have done?"

"Is the legend of the swords true though?" one asked. "Will they really strike dead one who touches them not of the blood of Chen Fei?"

She smiled at him. "There's a simple way to put it to the test if you don't believe." She made to offer him the hilt of her sword but he declined quickly.

"I am who I say I am. And if you have no reason to believe it, it should be enough that the shamans believe it. As you can see, they'll do anything to stop me. By my enemies you can judge me."

To this, they could give no argument. In truth though, she did not care what they believed. It was gold that interested them, and she could supply it. Whether she was of the blood of Chen Fei or not, that did not change. So they were content, though she did not doubt that if things went ill with her army they would tell the shamans they had been forced into cooperation.

It was a long evening. The gold was given to the city elders, and her army was billeted and fed. More than that, they were sheltered from the cold winter night. So far, so good.

Her forces now guarded key infrastructure and defensive positions. She had given orders for this because it meant nothing to have the protection of a fortified city like this if the enemy entered with the acquiescence of the populace. The elders had not been concerned by this, and all in all she did not fear betrayal from them. At least while her supply of gold held up.

She woke late the next morning and received news that did not surprise her. Overnight, the Nagrak force had besieged the town. At least as far as it was able to do so. They spread out below the cliffs, and there made themselves a camp that had the hallmarks of permanency. Latrines were being dug, tents for the commanders erected, and some earthwork had begun on a defensive wall to guard their front and side flanks.

Everything was as Shar expected, and yet something nagged at her. It was a gnawing fear, and it would not give her relief.

Later that morning, Boldgrim came to her where she surveyed the enemy from a balcony cut into the rock of the cliff that adjoined the living quarters she had been granted. He was never far away, being her guard against sorcerous attack, but he often stayed in the background while she spoke to scouts, generals and carried out the thousand and one daily tasks required of one who led such a large force.

"The enemy grow in number," he said. "Not just by the addition of warriors, but also by shamans. There are a half dozen now, and I expect more shortly."

How he knew she did not know. She trusted his assessment though, for it matched the growing anxiety she felt.

21. Show Me Now

"Why do the shamans not act?" Shar asked.

Boldgrim shook his head and offered no answer. There was none to give. They would attack when they chose to, and not before.

"They must be waiting for something," Radatan suggested.

Something about that rang true with Shar. They had no way of knowing inside the fortress what the shamans were planning. They could attack now if they wished. They outnumbered her and Boldgrim. It was the same thing with the Nagrak cavalry. They could have fought, but instead let Shar's army inside. All these decisions made sense, in a way.

Yet there was a pattern too. It had all been easy for her at every step. Perhaps that was just coincidence, but assuming so was dangerous. What if the enemy were operating to a plan?

She thought that through. If it were a plan, it would be one to their benefit. One that gave them an advantage, or one that gave them surprise.

There was no advantage for them in letting her hold the superior defensive position though. Unless they meant to trap her in the fortress city. That was possible, but they had given up an opportunity to defeat, or at least greatly weaken, her army first.

Her mind drifted to surprise. It was something she did well, and the enemy had shown little aptitude for it so far. This enemy commander was skilled though. He was one who might use it, if he had the opportunity.

151

There was nothing though. How could she be surprised inside a fortress?

"Think!" she said to herself.

The others glanced at her strangely. She had spoken aloud, but she ignored that. She was on the track of something now, and she kept pursuing the thought.

Perhaps the enemy had a plan. Perhaps they had a way to surprise her. If they could do it from within the city, that might be devastating.

It was possible the elders could turn on her. She did not think that was their intention though. Trust came slowly, but at the same time there was no reason to think they would betray her. Even if they did, her army was larger than theirs, by far, and now guarded all infrastructure. If they tried something, it would likely fail. And it was a slim hope for the Nagraks and the shamans. Better for them if they had tried to stop her entering the city in the first place.

There was no other way to surprise her from within the city though. They could not just magic their army inside. No, it was impossible.

What then was left? If they could not enter by magic, how else could it be done? The gate was guarded. It was the only entrance, and a bloody battle would be fought for anyone who tried to come that way. There was no other.

Shar shuddered. Suppose that was not true? Suppose there was another way, one that she did not know. The cave system was endless. The whole city was basically cut into the rock of the cliffs and hill that overlooked the river. Was it possible that a cave existed that offered a way in?

Her skin began to crawl. Of course it was possible. The elders need not even be complicit in treachery. Such a cave might be in disuse. Or sealed up and forgotten

152

generations ago. Yet the shamans had long memories. Some had been alive when her ancestor had built this city and designed its fortifications. Would he not have designed an escape route as well as defenses?

"We are in deadly peril," Shar said to those around her. She was surprised at the calmness in her voice.

They did not understand. Not yet. But to her, her realization of the danger might be too late. She left her rooms, an entourage around her, and hastened to the quarters of the first elder who lived nearby.

Coming to the door it was guarded, but only by one soldier. Evidently the ruling class of the city was popular with the people.

"I must see your master, and quickly," she said.

The soldier seemed somewhat taken aback by her urgency, but he entered the room and closed the door behind him. A few moments later he returned.

"Come this way," he instructed.

Shar and Boldgrim followed him into the room. The rest waited without. It would not be proper to take so many, unannounced, into the living quarters of the elder. He was, essentially, a chief, and she was already imposing on him by coming unannounced.

There were two other soldiers guarding the inside of the door, and an array of servants within. They were carrying out their tasks efficiently, but looked with curiosity upon Shar.

The soldier led them to a large couch, and invited them to sit.

"The master is currently having a bath. He will join you soon."

Shar stood again. "Young man, get him. Get him *now*. Or I'll go into his bathroom myself."

The soldier was out of his depth, but he looked once into her eyes and hurried away. Only a few moments later he returned, Rushkatar beside him, wet and covered only in a towel.

"This better be important," the elder said. He had a right to be irritated, but he was hiding it better than most would.

"Our lives depend on it," she replied.

"Get me a robe," he commanded one of his servants.

He looked at her then, and there was anger in his eyes. She liked that. Had he been part of any deception he would have tried much harder to smooth things over and delay.

"There's another way into the city," she said. "Through the caves. The Nagraks allowed me in here too easily, and now I've worked out why."

The servant gave him a robe, and once he hurriedly wrapped it around himself he let the towel fall to the floor.

"There's no other way into the city. Only the entrance you came through yourself."

"You are wrong," she said. "Think!"

He did not like that. "I believe I'm more familiar with the city than you are," he said sarcastically.

Shar ignored his tone. "You know the city, but I know Chen Fei. I know how he thought, and what he did throughout his life. I know him like I know myself. We both had the same teacher. And I *tell* you, he built the defenses here with an escape route in mind. Think! You must have heard something at some point. It may have been sealed off generations ago and forgotten, but it's there."

He made to speak, but then stopped himself. Instead, he sat down on the couch.

"The cave systems are endless. On top of that there are many hand-delved tunnels. The population is less now than what it has been at times during our history.

No one knows all the tunnels, or where they lead. Especially in the remote areas that few have cause to visit."

He sat in silence, thinking, but one of his servants approached. It was an old lady, and she bowed respectfully.

"My lord, may I speak? My grandmother told me a story of such a cave."

Shar's attention flashed onto the woman, but she did not speak. She waited then on Rushkatar, and watched him closely.

"Speak freely," the elder said. His reaction seemed natural to Shar, and she could detect no sign of annoyance as might have been the case if he were conspiring with the Nagraks.

"I was only a little girl," the old woman said. "We lived down at the lower levels, at the far north of the city." She glanced at Shar. "Those are the poor levels. There's no light, save what we make ourselves, and the air isn't fresh. It's deep underground, and old. Sometimes tunnels collapse, especially those closer to the river."

The woman spoke as though reminiscing, and not quickly enough for Shar. There would be a point to it though, Shar guessed, and held her impatience in check.

"That's what we believed had happened. One of my friends had gone missing, and it was thought she was lost in the tunnels. A search party was organized, but they didn't find her. They did find a place where a wall had come part down though. They shored it up, and ventured down that way. Eventually, they found my friend. She was happy as could be, and not scared at all. When she was asked if she had been afraid all alone in the dark, she shook her head. She told them she had just come back from playing in the sun by the river."

Shar felt her heart race. This was it. This was confirmation.

"Can you find that tunnel now?" she asked.

"Of course. It's as fresh as yesterday in my memory. The place where the wall was shored up is still visible, or it was. But they put a door there to keep any other children out."

Shar felt a wave of fear rising through her. Already the enemy may have infiltrated the city. There could be hundreds, perhaps thousands of soldiers pouring in like a river emptying into a lake.

"Show us. Take us there now, as fast as you can walk."

They followed her out the room, and Shar whispered instructions to Asana.

"Gather soldiers as we go. Our own if you can get them. Get as many as you can, and send word for more to follow us."

They hastened along the corridors. Rushkatar, still in his robe, gathered some of his own men. Soon a throng of them hurried forward, and they followed the old lady who could still walk at a fair pace.

Down they went, and it grew darker. Lanterns were less common, and there were fewer people. Those they saw avoided them, fearing so many soldiers at once in a place they seldom came.

Shar lost track of the stairways they descended, and the long sloping tunnels. Some were natural caves, but more were delved by hand.

The air grew stifled, and soon they left all areas of habitation. The corridor the old lady led them down was dark as night, but there were wooden torches stacked in the last real room and they lit many of these and pressed ahead.

Shar held a flaming brand in one hand, and in her other one of her swords. The old woman looked at her, fear in her eyes now, her step faltering.

"Forward," Shar commanded. "No harm will come to you."

They came to a narrow corridor, and there they found a door of dilapidated timber. It was open, but there was no sign of anyone.

Shar took the lead now. There seemed only one tunnel, but the old woman was close by. So was Asana and the men he had found along the way. One was even a Fen Wolf, and Shar recognized him. He grinned at her in the semi dark.

They shuffled ahead. The way was narrow, and few soldiers could come at any one time. That was good. If they met the enemy, it would be easier to hold them. But if they came in great enough numbers they could still push through. And that was supposing they were coming this way at all. What if this was a false lead?

Shar gritted her teeth and swept her hair back in vexation. She could not be everywhere at once. This was the information she had, and she had to trust to it that it was right.

The air seemed dead now, and the walls were not just rock but sometimes partly of clay. It was dangerous to go further. She had the feeling that the ceiling could collapse at any time. It was more dangerous to stop though. If they did not find where the enemy intended to come in, they were all dead.

She put from her mind the thought that the enemy were already here. Perhaps ahead somewhere, or maybe coming up some other way. For all she knew fighting might already have broken out in the upper levels.

The torches seemed to cast less light, and she wondered if the air was even more stifling than she thought. It was not so. She soon saw that the tunnel was widening, and there was simply not enough light to cover the larger space.

They came to an intersection. To the left, the tunnel descended at a deeper angle into the dark. It was almost like a pit. To the right, it climbed steadily upward.

Shar thought of asking the old woman which way to go, but she had fallen behind in the dark somewhere, and she had never been this far anyway.

There she halted deep in thought, and the others pressed closely around her. She did not have enough soldiers yet to go both ways. One must be chosen, and only a very small group could be left behind to watch the other.

22. This Is My Task

Shar felt frustration well up in her. "I'd give ten thousand in gold for a dwarven miner right now."

No one answered. There was no dwarven miner to tell her what to do, or what tunnel would be used for what. Why did one go up and the other down?

She felt that she knew Chen Fei though, and how he thought. Shulu had taught her, in detail, every one of his campaigns. His successes and his failures. She must put that knowledge to use.

"Each of these tunnels lead somewhere," she said. "They're man-made, so they have a purpose."

"We've been going down a long time," Huigar replied. "If one of them leads to a concealed entrance outside, maybe it's time we started moving back up."

There was truth in that. It was the larger and more finished tunnel too. She had been wrong a moment ago though. She had assumed each path led away somewhere, but she was looking at that the wrong way. Just as likely they in fact led *to* this place not *away* from it.

Which perspective was right?

The weight of pressure bore down on her. If she chose badly, all could be lost. Her hand brushed the hilt of one of her swords, and she had an idea. It was almost a compulsion. What did anything matter though, if the swords could help?

In a swift motion she dropped her torch and drew the blades, holding them before her face. They glittered in the firelight, dark as though they absorbed all light, yet giving off their own dark shimmers.

She felt their power. She sensed that which was in them, and spoke.

"Hail, O swords of Dawn and Dusk. Answer my call."

A voice rang from the sword, cold and strong. "Hail, sister."

A shiver ran through her at the word sister, and in the flickering light she saw the others step back from her, some with fear on their faces. She ignored it all. Only the information the swords could provide was of importance.

"Which tunnel leads to the outside?" she asked. "Which way should I go?"

"O sister, I feel your anguish. Would that I could aid you. Yet I know little of human history, and none of this place you call Tashkar. Follow your heart, and rejoice, for whatever you choose I will fight with you at the end. And that comes soon."

Shar wanted to scream. Instead, she sheathed the blades again and ignored the dismay around her.

What would Chen Fei have been thinking? There would be an escape route. Not for the whole city because that was impossible. For the leadership, perhaps. Or women and children, maybe. Or to send or receive secret messengers. Yet once they came out on the river flats they would likely be discovered by enemy scouts. So escape would be very difficult even if they could get out of the city.

Unless …

"I have it!" she said. "We'll go down. Let five remain here to guard the upper tunnel, and choose one as a runner to give warning above if the enemy comes down it."

"Why down?" Asana asked. He said nothing of the swords, but she knew that was on his mind.

"Where better to escape to than the river? Boats could be hidden there, and they would allow getting away, or approaching unseen. Either way, it offers protection from scouts on the grassland."

His eyes widened a little at that, and she took that for a good sign. It was a simple answer, but it made a lot of sense.

They moved forward now, and Shar was in the lead, torch held high again. A part of her wanted to run, but to do so might be to blindly stumble into enemy forces. At the same time, if she hurried, she might find the exit and secure or demolish it before ever the enemy could use it.

It was not like her to be caught in two minds, but caution won out. She led them forward more slowly, and signaled for absolute silence. That way she might at least detect the enemy before they detected her.

The tunnel seemed sinister to her. Shadows leaped and squatted along the damp walls, and the floor underneath grew increasingly damp. At times there was actual loose water. She wondered if they could go on much farther, for the walls looked ready to collapse and smother them all in mud.

Even as they passed through the worst of it, they came to a set of stone stairs. It was a kind of bridge, made by the hands of ancient craftsmen and rarely used, but still performing its function. Below them was the murmur of running water in the dark, and then they were over it and to the other side.

The tunnel ran upward now, and Shar moved forward. Despite traversing higher ground, the walls became no dryer, and often drops of moisture, beading on the ceiling, dripped down.

Something scuttered in the dark ahead. Shar did not see it clearly, but she knew what it was.

"Only a rat," she whispered.

161

Onward she went, and she passed the torch to someone behind her and drew her swords. Surely now they must be getting close to the exit.

Hope grew in her that she was on time. She had gotten here before the Nagraks. Unless they were coming another way...

The floor grew even damper, and her footfall made a splash in a puddle of water. Looking down, the whole floor was wet, but the torches were far enough back now that the light was not strong and it was difficult to see. Her eyes were adjusting though, and she thought she could detect something ahead.

She was right. The tunnel was widening, and they came to some sort of cavern. There were ancient timber benches here, half rotted because of the moisture. Some had collapsed. Others still stood. On those one were pots and the remains of bags. There were also chairs and blankets, though the latter, when not rotted, had been torn apart and used in rats' nests, of which there were many. There was a smell of rot in the air too, and Shar believed many of the bags had once contained grain.

"This is a staging area," she whispered to Asana. "Food and supplies were stored here in case a quick escape was needed and there was no time to gather them in the upper levels."

The swordmaster nodded in the dark, his eyes keen with a sense of excitement. It was said that he could sometimes foretell the future. So the stories went anyway. It was nothing more than a rumor hinted at, yet his eyes had an intense but faraway look and he fingered the ring that marked him as abbot.

Something else struck her as strange. The few remaining monks who followed him from Nashwan Temple were always silent, staying in the shadows. She had not even known they were in this group down here in the deeps of the earth, but almost like they sensed something themselves, or Asana's manner had informed them, they had come to the fore now, standing close to their leader.

The room was circular, and timber beams stood upright in several places, holding a framework of rafters above. Some of the beams and rafters had rotted through and fallen. Others remained precariously in place. There were no other doors or paths. Ahead though, the one that had led them here continued on, narrow again.

Even the torchlight did little to relieve the gloom, and if ever there were a dolorous place it was this. It seemed almost like a tomb. Shar gathered herself, and was about to step forward when she heard a noise. It was faint, but after a moment she realized what it was. The splash of a foot in water. Not from one of the men with her, but from the shadows of the tunnel opposite.

"Charge!" she cried out and sprang forward.

If only she could prevent the enemy from coming into this larger chamber it would be so much easier to hold them back until more help arrived. Even as she ran though, soldiers came out of the passageway's mouth like ants from a nest.

She saw a face she knew, and stumbled. It saved her life. A spear flew through the air where she had been, and it struck a man behind her. She was up and slashing with her sword a moment later, too close now for more missiles.

The man she had engaged died, his throat torn out by the tip of the Sword of Dawn, and she swung her head around. The familiar face was gone, lost somewhere in the crowd of combatants, but she would know Bai-Mai anywhere. The monk had allied himself with the

163

Nagraks, and no doubt still sought the ring Asana now wore.

A shabby tribesman swung at her with an axe, an unusual weapon for a Nagrak, and she swayed to the side and ran him through. With a kick at his body she withdrew her blade, and whipped it up into the face of another attacker.

It was chaos in the cavern. Screams rang out, and the clash of sword on sword was deafening in the enclosed space.

Shar's group was pushed back by the ferocity of the fighting. It might be wise to withdraw to the narrower tunnel down which they had come, but the fighting was in the balance. To try to change now might be to give the enemy momentum to carry home the attack and rout the defenders, even in the narrow tunnel.

She fought on, both swords whirling through the air and bringing death. The enemy swiftly grew wary of her, avoiding her where possible. This gave her a moment to survey the melee.

It still hung in the balance. Yet Asana was there, and his thin blade moved so fast it was barely seen. The dead piled up around him, and the enemy avoided him too.

"Forward!" commanded Shar. She knew opportunity when she saw it. The fight was in the balance, but the Nagraks, avoiding her and Asana, were at a momentary disadvantage. As the two of them tired they would be less lethal, and the advantage would swing back the other way. Now was the time to capitalize on the situation. Now, or perhaps never.

She led by example. Shuffling forward, swords flashing before her. Huigar and Radatan were close by. They tried to protect her, but that was impossible. You could not protect a fighter out in front.

Shar pushed harder. She sensed this was the moment, and determination drove her. To some her action might have seemed reckless, but it was the safest course in the long run.

A half dead man who lay on the ground stabbed at her with a knife. The blade gashed her calf, but it was only a glancing blow. She leaped over him, and even as she did so she saw out of the corner of her eye Huigar thrust downward with her sword.

The chamber was full of the dead and dying now. Yet most of them were the enemy. Fear gripped the remainder of the enemy, and they began to retreat. The way was narrow though, and many died as they tried to scramble through.

To Shar's surprise, the end was sudden. Most of the enemy were dead, or had fled back down the tunnel. By the luck of the gods she had determined their plan in time, and stymied it. If their force had come through to the upper levels unchallenged, chaos would have broken out. The end would have been quick, for they would have built up large numbers in the lower levels before they made their attack. That had been prevented, at least for now.

Reinforcements would be on the way. Soon these tunnels would be blocked, and probably an engineer would know how to collapse them. The plans of the shamans would be in ruin with them.

They must keep the enemy at bay for a little while longer though. No doubt they would have reinforcements coming too, and soon. She made for the tunnel opposite, and her blood ran cold. The last of the defenders was there, sword before him and the blade running red with blood.

It was Bai Mai. She saw in her mind how he had callously killed the old abbot, and anger stirred in her blood as well as fear. He had enormous skill, but if he died the enemy would lose morale. If he held the entrance though, they might rally behind him and try to break through again. This time with even greater numbers.

She strode toward him, and she felt the malice of his gaze as he watched her and readied himself.

"Halt!" The cry was loud and commanding. It was Asana, and his call echoed through the cavern. "This is my task."

They were simple words, but to her amazement Shar felt even greater fear. It was one thing to face death herself. It was another to let Asana fight this man who might have even greater skill. He was an opponent such as even the swordmaster had not faced before.

23. The Skill of Gods

Shar was still as a mountain. It seemed the weight of the earth pinned her down, and she was not sure if she could move even if she wanted to. Such was the force of Asana's will.

He was Asana Gan. Even she felt his authority, when he chose to display it, as he did now.

The swordmaster walked quietly through the defenders and faced Bai-Mai. He lifted up his left hand, and the ring of the abbot on his finger caught the firelight.

Bai-Mai hissed. "You taunt me with that which is mine by right?"

"Taunt you? No. Fate has brought us together for a different purpose. I, Asana Gan, proclaim you guilty of the crimes of treason and murder. You defiled the Nashwan Temple, and caused its destruction. You turned brother against brother, and their deaths are your fault. Master Kaan, you murdered. For these crimes, you will be put to death."

Bai-Mai seemed unaffected. "Justice is all well and good, but those are empty words. You have no power to enforce them."

"Have I not?"

Asana drew his slender sword. It rang as it came from the sheath, and Shar thought she saw lights glimmer within it. It was said the souls of Asana's ancestors rested in the blade. Even Shulu had not been sure of that, or chose to keep knowledge of such magic to herself.

"We will fight," the swordmaster said. "The two of us alone. None will interfere. Justice will prevail. If you say no to this, then all will see you are a coward."

Bai-Mai stepped into the chamber, blood dripping from his sword.

"I am no coward. I am your better. To me have been transmitted the full secrets of the temple, while you wandered the land and wasted your promise."

Asana gave no answer. The two of them circled each other, stepping with deft grace, their bodies supple as a stalking cat's.

Bai-Mai struck first. Shar barely saw it, but his blade thrust forward like a viper's tongue. It would have killed many a soldier who would not have deflected it in time, but Asana was no ordinary warrior. He did not even deflect it, but merely rocked his weight onto his back leg and created distance from the point.

They went back to circling. Bai-Mai was taller, and so had a longer reach. He had spent all his life at the temple, so he had received more training. Shar feared for Asana. Yet he *had* wandered the land, and he had fought much and been exposed to different combat strategies. That was a practical advantage to him.

Suddenly there was a blur of blades and steel rang out, sparks flying from the metal in the semi dark.

The two combatants parted, neither having been wounded nor showing any distress. What would have killed most men was merely a testing of skill for them. And so far as Shar could see, they had been equal.

Bai-Mai looked fierce, his eyes flashing with emotion. Asana was calm as a summer's day, yet there was something in his eyes that spoke of determination, and she knew that even if he were killed, in death he would bring his enemy down with him.

Without warning Asana struck. It was a low sweeping blow at his opponent's ankle, but the other nimbly leaped back and laughed.

"You're slower than you were in your youth."

"Am I? Or do I merely wish you to think so?"

It was a good reply. It cast doubt in the opponent's mind, and even as Bai-Mai must have been distracted considering it, Asana attacked again. This time it was an overhead strike followed by lateral slashes. The speed of each stroke was stunning, and few even among great warriors could have reacted in time to fend them off. Shar was not sure she was good enough, but Bai-Mai seemed no more put off than before. Almost lazily he deflected the strokes, though he did retreat.

"Better," the monk said. "But not good enough. You are old and easy prey as was Master Kaan. Shall I show you what true speed is?"

He waited on no reply. Employing the same tactic of distraction as Asana had, he drove forward, sword flashing like light reflecting from a broken mirror.

Asana retreated. His every move was lithe and unrushed. He seemed casual as though on a morning stroll in a garden, and relaxed as a cat lying in the winter's sun.

The swordmaster grew more relaxed as he retreated, often not even bothering to deflect a blow but letting it pass by within inches of his body. When he did deflect, there was barely even the clash of blade against blade. He seemed in command and at ease, and many in the chamber gasped.

The skill was astonishing. Both men fought with the skill of gods. Yet Asana was not quite as quick. He was more deft though, and the battle that played out was equal.

169

Bai-Mai did not like it. His eyes flashed with anger and emotions played across his face. In that, they were not equal at all. Asana remained tranquil, and he fought with a different style. He battled as one who merely played a game, not caring or even thinking of the outcome. He merely reacted. Bai-Mai fought like a demon.

The fight spilled out toward the center of the chamber, and their struggles were cast as giants by the torchlight across the walls. Shar could not take her eyes from it. She knew she should guard against the enemy regrouping and coming through the tunnel again, but she could not draw her gaze away from a friend that she loved who fought for his very life.

Back and forth the combatants contended, one having an advantage and pressing it, then the other in turn doing the same.

Shar realized she was not a match for either of them. Asana had saved her life, and his skill was greater even than she had known. Only now, being tested by an equal, did he display it.

She learned something too. Both of them always seemed to have the tip of their sword pointing at the heart of their opponent. Not only did it help protect them, but it meant that should the enemy falter at any moment one step and a quick thrust would end the fight in death.

Death did not come though. So close were they matched, even if in different ways, that no advantage lasted more than a few moments before the other exploited a weakness.

Bai-Mai dropped low and struck at Asana's knees. The swordmaster stepped back, but Bai-Mai skipped forward, his sword arcing high and coming down in a great overhand strike. Asana blocked it, but he was not as quick as he had so often been before. This time it was not a deflection but a blow of force against force.

The swords clashed in a shower of sparks and with a screech one of the blades broke. At first, Shar was not sure which it was, then she saw Asana bring his blade to point at the enemy again.

Bai-Mai cast his hilt at Asana, who easily dodged it.

"Even your sword refuses to serve you. Thus it was with the people of Skultic also. You have fallen to serving the shamans," Asana taunted.

Bai-Mai grew red in the face, but he said nothing. Asana stepped back a few paces, and Shar saw he came to her. He handed her his sword, and she felt that the hilt was hot and sensed something of the magic that was in it. It was of a kind entirely different from that in her own blades, but she felt it nonetheless.

"Be careful," she whispered.

"What will be, will be as it must."

The swordmaster walked back toward Bai-Mai. They took up their fight again, only this time it was hand to hand. The stories always spoke of Asana and his sword, but the monks trained in unarmed combat before ever they touched a weapon. Some specialized in it.

Again the two combatants circled each other. Again their movements, when one attacked and one defended, were swift as thought. Bai-Mai struck with a hammer fist, dropping his weight into the blow. Asana eased back into a cat's stance, kicking at the other's groin.

Neither blow landed, but then they launched into a series of strikes too swift to follow. After a loud thud though, Asana staggered to the side. Bai-Mai had caught him a blow on the ribs.

Asana fell back under a rain of blows, many the hammer hand technique that Bai-Mai seemed to like. Yet even as he retreated he hooked out with his foot and

171

caught the oncoming step of his opponent, pulling it out from under him.

Bai-Mai fell forward. Asana let drop his own hammer hand and it struck the monk's shoulder as he dodged sideways. There was yet another thud, and a muffled cry.

The two separated again, and paused to take their breath.

Even as the two enemies watched each other with wary suspicion, Shar heard noise behind her. A quick glance told her all she needed to know. Reinforcements had finally arrived, and Tashkar was safe from infiltration by the enemy. She let out a sigh, and knew that by the grace of the gods she had prevented catastrophe, if only by the slenderest of margins.

The relief she should have felt though eluded her. Asana still faced a deadly opponent, and she was not sure he would win. If he died, she vowed that Bai-Mai would next have to face her.

Asana held up his left hand, and the abbot's ring, the sign of his authority, gleamed once more.

"We have played enough, you and I. But I weary of this game. The time for justice has come, for as you lived so shall you die."

"Empty words," Bai Mai replied. As he spoke he skipped forward and then leaped, his feet shooting out in a double kick. Asana sidestepped, seeming to have all the time in the world.

Bai-Mai landed on his feet, pivoted and launched a blistering attack of both hands and feet. Asana barely moved and yet he somehow avoided all the blows, and then his arms snatched a punch of Bai-Mai's in the very air, one hand above the elbow and the other just above the wrist. With a turn of his waist he broke his opponent's arm.

Bai-Mai screamed and fell to his knees, his arm hanging at an unnatural angle. With a cry of rage he sprang to his feet again and kicked at Asana.

The swordmaster rocked back out of the way and then pounced forward, his hands clasping each side of Bai-Mai's head.

A moment the two men stood together, seemingly motionless as they strove against one another. Bai-Mai sought to drop his weight and escape the terrible grip. Asana strove to counter him and find the right angles. A moment only it was. Less than the blink of an eye, and then Asana acted.

Shar knew what was coming. She had seen it done to Master Kaan by Bai-Mai. She saw in this the symmetry of justice. There was a sudden jerk by Asana. The weight of his whole body was in it, and the head of Bai-Mai twisted with a crack between the swordmaster's hands. The noise of it was like a whip cracking in the underground chamber.

His neck broken, Bai-Mai kicked out involuntarily with one leg and then crumbled. Almost gently Asana let him down to the ground, where he lay dead.

Atachi! cried the monks. It was not a word in use among the Fen Wolf tribe, but Shar could surmise its meaning. *Vengeance through justice.*

The monks gathered around Asana. What they said Shar could not hear, but they spoke to the swordmaster. While they did, Asana knelt and closed the eyelids of his enemy.

The chamber was full of people, and there were many more behind in the tunnel. Shar must act quickly, but she waited for Asana to come over to her.

She handed him his sword, hilt first as was proper among warriors, her fingers brushing his hand as she let the weapon go.

173

"Justice is done, Asana Gan, and abbot. Master Kaan can now rest in peace."

"So I hope."

Shar moved quickly then. By luck she had foiled this attempt on the city, but the tunnel must still be closed off before a greater force of Nagraks entered it.

24. Uneasy At Heart

Shar sent two scouts along the tunnel ahead. They returned swiftly, declaring the passageway was full of the enemy and they were approaching.

"Were there any other offshoots from the main tunnel?" she asked.

"Not that we saw, and we believe we were close to the exit above ground."

An idea had occurred to Shar, and she was quick to implement it. They removed their own dead soldiers, and transported them with honor back toward the city. She was tired of death. Tired of all those who died in her name, and of the loss of those who perished for the shamans. But she hardened her heart for what was to come.

The enemy dead they left, including Bai-Mai. This chamber would be their tomb for eternity. At least if her plan worked. If not, they had warriors enough to hold the tunnel now until a different strategy could be devised.

A few prudent souls arriving with the reinforcements had brought ropes. These were tied to the bases of the wooden beams, and a few to the rafters that could be reached. Then the men withdrew into the tunnel behind them, drawing the ropes with them.

They did not have to wait long for the enemy. A few scouts came through first, and they secured the tunnel mouth. Soon many others came forward, filling up the chamber.

Shar called out from the dark of the tunnel opposite, where she had allowed shadowy movement to be seen to discourage the scouts from coming closer.

"You are not welcome here. This way is forbidden to you. Turn back, and live. Come forward, and die."

The enemy hesitated, uncertain. No doubt they could see the dead and knew a battle had been fought. And lost by them. They would have heard as much from the survivors as well.

It was clear they did not wish to proceed. They were Nagraks, used to fighting on horseback across green fields. This underground battle, on foot, in the dark, did not appeal. Yet orders were shouted from behind, and repeated.

The Nagraks came forward. Shar hardened her heart. She had given warning, and could do no more.

"Pull!" she cried, and hers were one of many pairs of hands holding a rope.

They pulled. The ropes lifted off the ground and went taut. The Nagraks were confused momentarily, and then some of them realized what was happening.

"Retreat!" was the cry from some.

"Charge!" commanded the leaders from the rear.

Chaos ensued, and a rope broke or else came free from the beam to which it was attached. Another worked, pulling down a small section of roof.

The screams were loud now, and all the enemy tried to retreat. Even as they turned their backs, more beams toppled. In one terrible moment the roof began to collapse, dust falling everywhere, rocks dislodging from above, and then with a terrible moan it all fell.

The chamber filled with screams. The air thickened with dust. A boom sounded as of thunder, and the earth trembled.

Shar was knocked down by the force of air that rushed up the tunnel with a moan, and she could barely breathe. Pulling her hood over her face, she turned her back to the catastrophe and struggled for air.

The screaming was silent now. But in its place came the sound of rushing water. The collapse of the chamber had broken a rock barrier somewhere, and all the fallen dirt was turning to mud.

Shar nearly vomited. There would yet be people alive under the rubble. Not all would have been killed by falling stones or beams. Now they spent their last moments alive in a hell of torment and fear. Because of her.

She ordered a withdrawal, but even as she did so the demon in the swords spoke, its voice ringing out loudly.

You glut me with death, sister. Praise to you. But more is to come, and my thirst shall not be slaked until the green Fields of Rah turn red.

The voice fell silent. Even in the semi dark Shar felt the eyes of the men upon her.

"Move!" she commanded. "This place isn't safe."

They moved, and quickly. Whether they feared more of the tunnel collapsing, the Swords of Dawn and Dusk, or her, she did not know. Whichever it was, they went farther back up the tunnel, but in several places where there were more beams, they collapsed those too.

At the last of these places Shar order a guard set. It was unlikely the enemy would try to dig their way through. And even if they did, it would be a desperate attempt likely to lead to more cave-ins and failure, but prudence dictated she guarded against the possibility.

The elders of the city greeted her and Rushkatar when she came to the surface again, and evidently they had heard word of all that transpired. They treated her with respect, and thanked her for what she had done, but there was a wariness in their eyes that disturbed her.

She glanced at Asana, close to her side as usual, and there was concern in his expression as well. The magic in the swords was growing in strength, and they all feared it.

She knew, even better than they, they were right to do so.

Later that night there was a celebration of the victory. She was shunned by many. Not because they did not believe in her but because they feared her. Only her friends stayed close, but even their glances held hints of trepidation.

Shar felt it too. Fear. Fear of the swords. Fear of the demon in them. At the same time, she needed the blades. Without their power, she would be dead. Without their magic, she would not beat the shamans.

Shulu had warned her of this. She had also said Chen Fei battled them as well. In the end, his power of will was greater than the demon's, but he was not unchanged by the contest. And at times his military strategies and the ravages of war that he unleashed were excessive.

What he could do, she could do. What he had done, she *must* do. The Cheng required it of her, and she would fulfill her duty, no matter what it was.

Music played around her, and there was dancing, smiles and polite conversation on the plaza beneath the stars that overlooked the river flats dusted with snow below. Shar felt the attraction of it all, but it was not her. She would rather be in Tsarin Fen by a campfire listening to the distant howl of a fen wolf.

She stayed close to the edge of the plaza, Asana nearby. There was a stone balustrade there, wreathed with multicolored lanterns and vines that grew in clay pots that gave forth a perfumed scent from their blossoms into the night.

"It's pretty," Asana said.

"It's not home," she replied.

To that he had no answer, and together they gazed out below.

The Nagrak army was hidden in the dark, but there were many campfires and around these the moving shadows of men.

"What disturbs you Shar? The swords?"

She did not look at him. "Yes, the swords. But something more. I feel a weight pressing down on me. I feel I'm in a trap, and the noose is tightening. Something else is happening. It will take place soon. I can feel it, but I don't know what it is."

Asana looked away from her and studied the army below, as did she.

"Whatever comes, we'll face it together."

She looked at him then, and smiled. "I'm lucky to have friends like you. I appreciate it."

A while longer she gazed out at the enemy, and then an idea occurred to her. She did not like to just wait. It was in her nature to stir things up, to get into the minds of her enemies and make them fear her. She gestured Boldgrim over, and the shaman eyed her warily.

"What can I do, Nakatath?"

"I would speak to the enemy. Amplify my voice so that it carries over the river flats."

"Now? During a party?"

"I don't think much of parties. Besides, it'll give these folk of Tashkar something to think about. They have invited a wolf into their home, and they should know that I'm no tame camp dog. Just in case they think they can control me."

179

He eyed her a moment, then shrugged. "Speak. Your words will be heard."

She still felt uneasy. Something had changed in the world, but she was not sure what. Maybe the shamans would know. They spoke at times with the gods, but the gods were capricious and the meaning of their words ever hard to interpret.

"You came against the city by stealth today," she said, and her voice rolled noisily down from the cliff face and over the flat lands. A hush descended behind her though on the plaza.

"You were beaten. You will always be beaten, for the Dark is nothing without Light. It is only shadow. But the Light can exist without Dark. The dreams of the shamans will become as dust. The iron shackles of their rule will crumble like ancient relics. Their day is done, and a new day dawns. The Cheng Empire will rediscover itself, and choose its own destiny."

It was a clear message. One to enrage the shamans, and to give the Nagrak sub-chiefs pause for thought. If they were too aligned with the shamans, they would be swept away with them. Most of all, it would give hope to ordinary people. The days of their servitude were drawing to a close.

The shamans acted quickly though. Not to be outdone they raised a figure of snow, and their sorcery swirled it together into a colossal form. It was in the image of a shaman: old, wise, hooded. And it looked at Shar, its eyes level with hers, and they were pits of darkness.

"Shar Fei, if that be your true name, you are no longer of the Light. The Dark is in your heart, and your deeds. We know your soul, and we understand that which now owns it. The Dark. A demon. You are a maelstrom of chaos and evil, and you will die. Just as did your forefather, if in truth you are of that accursed line."

Having spoken, the great figure fell to the ground, the sorcery that made it being withdrawn. The shamans would say no more this day, nor did they have to. She had thought to taunt them, to put them off balance as was ever her way. Instead, they had turned that taunting back on her. There were lies in their words, but there was truth also. She felt the sting of it.

Worse, she felt the gazes of all those on the plaza fall upon her, pondering. They would have heard rumors of her speaking to her swords. Or the swords speaking to her.

Now they knew she conversed with a demon.

25. An Age of Change

Shar felt a weight of oppression all night, and she did not sleep except for fitful spells that were worse than the waking hours. The next day dawned cold and bright. There were no clouds. The snow had mostly melted, and her heart was as lead.

It was not her normal mood. Always she found an outlook to any situation that gave her hope. While she had a goal to achieve, nothing could stop her. Toward that she worked and all else fell away from her mind.

Not today. Nor was there a good reason for this darkening of spirit. Not in a strategic sense. It was clear the enemy was going to attack. They were building toward it, and she sensed it coming imminently. Against the Nagrak horde though were strong defenses. She did not think it likely they could break through.

The shamans might throw their power against the city. If so, there was Boldgrim. And the Swords of Dawn and Dusk. Her swords. The demon blades that grew in power. It would be dark magic indeed that could overcome them.

Why then did she feel this sense of unease?

With a clenching of her fists she cast such thoughts aside. She watched the enemy from the same plaza as last night. From there she gave directions, and runners went back and forth. So too a series of men with horns were stationed at various locations to pass on any commands she gave. The army was growing used to her leadership style, and the methods she employed.

Tension built in the air. It was like a storm that brewed in the distance, cloud piling upon dark cloud and a teasing wind ahead of the billowing mass, hinting at what was to come.

A column of men coming in from the side drew her gaze.

"Who are they?" she asked.

"Perhaps reinforcements that arrived by boat," Radatan said. "They come from the river, and it is not entirely frozen over."

That was possible. But the Nagraks had little love of boats and traveled by horse. At least so Shulu had informed her.

It was possible this was some other tribe coming to help the Nagraks. Again though, the same question arose. Who would use boats?

She studied the column closely. It was challenged at times by Nagraks, but passed on without difficulty. It was a significant force of a thousand men, and so far as she could see their style of dress differed from one another.

"What tribe *are* they?" she asked. "They seem less like a tribe and more like a band of mercenaries."

The rest of her leadership group watched closely now as well, but they had no answers.

"Perhaps we shall see now," Huigar said, and she pointed to the head of the column.

Shar watched with growing curiosity. It looked like they were about to unfurl a large banner.

"Very strange," she muttered. "The shamans hate banners. It reminds the people they can be patriotic to something other than them."

The banner fluttered loose, and it was attached to two long poles, which were held up. Shar saw the design then, but she was not sure what to make of it. It showed a ship surging against the waves of the sea.

"Who *are* they?" she asked again.

The raising of their banner caused some problems. The Nagraks did not like it, but the column marched forward toward the path that led into the city.

An element of the Nagraks attacked the rear of the column, and were fended off. Confusion broke out amid the enemy, and the column surged forward.

Shar understood. At last. "Quickly! To the portcullis!"

She raced through the city and down to the lower levels. Many came with her.

"It is a trick!" Boldgrim said. "You can't mean to let them in?"

"I don't think so!" Shar yelled as she ran, and she did not have time to explain. Coming to the portcullis she found some Tashkar soldiers there, but most were her own and it was a force of several hundred.

"Lower the ramp! Prepare to charge out! We fight not the column but the Nagraks behind it!"

It could have been a moment of great confusion, but her men were well trained. More importantly they trusted her judgement, and they followed her orders without question.

The great contraption that was the portcullis, a mechanism of huge beams and bars of steel, lowered with a clamor of thunder. Out charged Shar, twin swords flashing and a host behind her. She negotiated the narrow and dangerous pathway, and came up to the approaching column.

The column was beset now by Nagraks, and Shar's force rushed into them. The enemy gave way and retreated, then rallied as some commander put iron into their will. The fighting was fierce. But such was the force

184

of Shar's onrush, and the surprise of it, that the Nagraks fell back.

"Now!" cried Shar. "Retreat into the city!"

The column, joined with her own men, did so. She fought a rearguard against the Nagraks who were regrouping, and the ravine before the portcullis became a killing field.

Shar rushed into the gathering enemy, her soldiers coming with her. She darted to the side to avoid a spear thrust, ran a man through and turned to decapitate the spearman.

The enemy were thickening. Most of the column was now inside the city, but the Nagraks had a chance to enter while the portcullis was down, if they moved quickly and decisively.

Her own men within the city acted faster. A deadly hail of arrows fell from above, the sky darkening with shafts. It was more than the Nagraks were prepared for, and they retreated. Even so, the order came from behind them to charge. Horns sounded desperately.

It was too late. Shar, and those remaining with her, used the opportunity of confusion to enter the city. Behind them, massive chains rattling, the portcullis was raised again. It was a barrier that defied the enemy, and cast humiliation at them as well as arrows.

Grudgingly, the Nagraks retreated. Shar heard their curses and laughed, for joy was upon her. Another thousand had joined her cause, and through the teeth of the enemy themselves had passed into her service.

The men about her were mostly from this new column, and she studied them as she walked through. They were hard men. They were mercenaries, of a kind, for they belonged to no one tribe. She saw many clans represented, but the one thing they all were was seamen. She saw it in the way they walked, the jaunty caps they wore to shield them from the sun and the rope callouses on their hands.

She looked for their leader, for one there must be. And she knew who it was.

His voice came from behind her, out of the midst of the men he had gathered in her name.

"See, Shar Fei, I keep my promises."

She spun around, saw him, and rushed forward to embrace him. He hugged her back fiercely.

"It seems like so long ago," she said.

"To me, it was but yesterday."

"How did you get these men, Captain Tsergar?"

He looked around at his comrades. "They are from here and there. From all over, really. Trade is slow at the moment, what with the war going on. Many were out of jobs, so it was easy to recruit."

"And how did you know to find me here?"

"Word of you is on all the lips in the land. We were heading to Nagrak City, but only yesterday heard you were here."

Boldgrim came over, studying the new man whom Shar seemed so friendly with. There was curiosity in his eyes.

"This is Captain Tsergar," she said. "I met him on the north coast, escaping Chatchek Fortress when I retrieved the swords. He took me toward the Wahlum Hills."

"He knew who you were, even then?"

"He knew, and he kept my secret. For secret it was then. He could have turned me in before ever I had an army."

Boldgrim shook his hand. "You bring a thousand swords, and that is no small thing. They are needed."

The captain bowed. "I do my part, as do the men, for Nakatath. They are tough men all, and good in a fight.

They are better with knives than fighting battles with swords though."

"We'll train them," Shar said. "And feed them and pay them. They'll not regret their service."

"And will they be on the winning side in the end?"

"Things go well," Shar answered. "So far at least. The noose tightens around the neck of the shamans, but there's still a long way to go."

The new band of men were welcomed into the city and housed in underground barracks. Tsergar, by the amount of men he had brought, his experience and Shar's trust in him, joined her leadership group.

A night of merriment ensued, and the city, so the elders said, thrived as it had in olden times. The centuries had seen its decline, both in wealth and population. Now, it was as it must have been in the time of Chen Fei.

Shar slept uneasily, her hands searching for the hilts of her swords even in slumber. These days, she never rested well, but it was particularly so now. The Nagraks had been made fools of by a column of soldiers that they thought had come to help them. There would be an attack. Soon.

By dawn, Shar was up and she watched as the sky lightened and the enemy were revealed. The plaza, situated high in the middle of the cliff face was a perfect place for her to command from. She had a good view of everything, and all the defenses were within easy reach.

"They will come against us today," she said, her arms resting on the stone balustrade.

"If they do, they'll die in great numbers," Asana said. He was close to her, as always lately. She knew why. He watched for signs that the swords controlled her.

"Their plans have fallen into chaos. They counted on coming up through the caves unchallenged. That failed.

Tsergar's entry into the city humiliated them. They *will* attack. Send word for all to be ready."

She looked around for Boldgrim. He was close too, and no doubt for the same reason as Asana.

"They'll use magic today. The shamans will try to win by the best means at their disposal. They know swords alone won't do it, and that trying to win that way will lead to a heavy loss of morale. Are you ready?"

The shaman gave the slightest of nods. He was tense, and he felt what she did. The enemy would assault them with everything they had, and try to regain the initiative.

So it came to pass. Within the hour the Nagraks, on foot, attacked the narrow way to the portcullis. At the same time, they swarmed the cliffs as well using poles and ladders to try to enter the city.

Their losses were massive. A hail of arrow shafts darkened the sky and the killing ground before the portcullis lived up to its name.

The men with poles and ladders fared no better. They too were killed by arrow, but more were simply dashed to their deaths below by the dislodging of the timber up which they clambered.

"Get ready!" Shar said. "This is but a feint."

Even as she spoke the air seemed to turn cold. A sizzling sound rose up from somewhere below, and jagged lightning leaped upwards.

Shar expected something of the kind. The magic in her swords flared to life, and light burst from them, streaking through the air to tangle the lightning. Fire and smoke roiled in the sky before Tashkar, and then fell to earth in a cloud of ash.

Again the shamans struck. This time they hurled lightning at the other side of the city. Boldgrim raised both arms above his head, and a shield appeared.

188

Lightning struck the dome of light, and the stone beneath Shar's feet trembled.

When it was done, and the magic dissolved back into the air, Boldgrim hurled his own lightning. He was careful not to strike at Nagraks, but instead at the group of shamans, as always, behind their army.

This the shamans must have expected. They raised their own shield, a seething cloud of crimson and wicked green. It did not batter away the attack, but absorbed it. Then with a pulse, lightning shot from it.

The attack came straight at Shar. She stood her ground while others near her ran to the sides. The swords of power she lifted high, the beloved blades that protected her, and from them came a howl as though from a wolf in the wild. Even as the noise sounded, light sprang from the steel.

Immediately, Shar saw that the light took the form of a great wolf, jaws open, with a silvery mane, thick and regal, about its neck. Into those wide-open jaws the attack streaked. And was swallowed.

The wolf ceased howling. A little higher than man tall it was, and it was uncanny to see the shimmering form, massive, vaporish, standing in the air only, begin to growl.

The beast shook itself like a dog dislodging water from its pelt, and a hundred shards of magic flew like sparks down at the Nagrak army. This caused dismay among them, killing those it hit and setting fire to supplies, equipment and men alike.

It was unlawful for a shaman to use magic against mere warriors. In this the shamans had broken a sacred tenet of Cheng culture. Shar knew the same might be said of her, but she did not care. She had defended rather than attacked. Nor was she a shaman.

189

The wolf leaped down, landed on the ground far below, and even as it did so it transformed and grew in stature. This was beyond Shar's knowledge, and though Shulu had said the magic would strengthen, and that it would respond differently to her than to her forefather, nothing prepared her for this.

An image of light stood now before the city, towering high. It was a warrior, and it looked like Shar. Twin swords were in its hands, and violet lightning crowned its head.

Even the shamans cowered at that. On the head was a horned helm, and the aspect of the figure was terrible to behold. If helm it was. It occurred to Shar that the image was part her, and part demon. She hoped no one noticed that.

The Nagraks retreated. It was not clear that the shamans wanted that, but they were lost to view as the massive army fell back. It did not flee though. It merely repositioned itself.

The image of light strode forward, massive swords flashing. With an effort of will that brought sweat to her face, Shar sheathed the Swords of Dawn and Dusk. She did not think the Nagraks would continue their attack, and the shamans had met their match. They would not either until there were more of them.

The image turned toward Shar, eyes blazing, and then it fell apart like mist before a breeze.

A hush fell over the field. The Nagraks made no move. Nor, as might be expected, did the defenders cheer their victory. They had won, but they were not sure how. She knew what they were thinking though. They distrusted magic. They wondered what the origin of hers was. And some guessed it was demonic.

There was nothing she could do. What would be, would be. Had she not controlled the magic though?

That should count for something. Likewise, beggars could not be choosers. If the people wanted freedom from tyranny, it would come at a cost. They could not expect otherwise.

Shar turned to speak to Asana, but his eyes were not looking at her. Instead, they were turned skyward.

Following the swordmaster's gaze, she looked for what he saw. At first, she saw nothing. Then she spotted a black dot in the sky. It was a bird. Soon she saw it was a raven, and it drifted down toward the high plaza on which she stood in lazy circles.

There was muttering all around her. Something did not seem normal about this bird. And ravens, after all, were associated with the gods and sometimes served as their messengers.

Or presaged their appearance. Shar could almost hear her grandmother's instructional voice in her head now.

The bird drifted lower, and the black of its feathers turned to white. It landed deftly upon the stone balustrade, and there it became a vision of light too bright to look upon.

Shar shielded her eyes. To her ears came a sense of elusive music, tranquil, strong and stern all at once. When she looked again the light had become the image of a woman.

Nor just any woman. It was the visage of Uhrum, Queen of the gods. She was clad in white and wore a golden belt around her waist. Upon her brow rested a circlet of beaten gold. Her glorious hair streamed back into the air behind her, gold also, but colored with a ruddiness like the embers of a fire. And then there were the double horns on her head, curving back like a ram's.

Shar curtsied as Shulu had taught her, and the goddess let the gaze of eons uncounted fall upon her. Shar met that gaze, though she swallowed.

191

Uhrum spoke, and her voice was as music in the air drifting from afar, yet still clear.

"Your fight is just, Shar Fei. Know, however, that other powers in the world are at play also, older than shamans and humanity."

Shar thought quickly. Elves and dwarves were older than humanity, but so were gods and demons. It was the latter to which she thought Uhrum referred.

"It is an age of transformation," the goddess went on. "Time and space have reached an eddy where what once was reaches out toward what could yet be. The demons that in times past ruled the world seek the power they had before they were cast out."

The goddess paused, and her gaze was fierce, flickering with light as strong as the sun's.

"That must not be." She turned her full gaze on Shar, and it smote her with power. "Better to die than allow that."

Shar straightened. She felt the awe of the goddess envelop her, but she did not step back. Even so, she felt in her heart the truth of the words uttered. Better to die than allow demons dominion over the world. And she knew those words were directed at her, and why.

She understood. Shar bowed her head in acknowledgement, and sorrow flooded her. Then she let it flow away. What must be must be, and her death to prevent the demons controlling her through the swords was a small price to pay for saving the Cheng people from tyranny.

The goddess ceased speaking, and the people of Tashkar began to sing a hymn. It was not one that Shar knew, but she had heard the like before.

Soon the singing ceased, and Uhrum reached out and placed a hand on Shar's head. A blessing some might call it. Being prepared for death others might say. But under

192

the influence of the goddess's touch she began to sing herself, and knew it for divine prophecy.

Her voice was strong and clear, for she had sung many times to Shulu, if rarely to others. Uhrum withdrew a step, and Shar opened up her arms and gazed about her at all the defenders of the city.

Slivered hangs the moon in the sky
Fast and sleek the barbed arrows fly
My heart to pierce with iron fierce
To lay me low in dust to die.

The shamans rule with fear and fire
My challenge sparks their deadly ire
For freedom I fight against their might
My blood to build a new empire.

Facing fire-whips and darkling spells
By light of star beneath the fells
Shamans I'll fight and win despite
My fate to die as doom foretells.

Slivered hangs the moon in the sky
Fast and sleek the poison arrows fly
My heart to pierce with venom fierce
To lay me low in dust to die.

The shamans rule the cowered lands
All things wither beneath their hands
What once was green no more is seen
So flash our swords like fiery brands!

Against their might with steel we'll crash
Our swords to cut their tyrant's lash
Freedom to win in battle din

Until they fall in fire and ash.

Through the cavern the wild wind moans
Beneath my feet the mountain groans
Smoke and red fire, chaos and spells dire
Crack cave walls and cast crashing stones.

Sorcerous hangs the moon on high
Fast and sleek the wicked arrows fly
My heart they pierce with malice fierce
Bury me deep, beneath the sky.

Her words drew to an end, and the city was silent. She saw tears on the faces of her friends. They understood what she had spoken under the influence of the goddess. She would not survive the final battle. That did not mean the shamans would win though.

Uhrum, Queen of the Gods, bowed as she faded away.

Shar stood tall. She would die. Everyone knew it now, but they thought it was the shamans who would kill her. Perhaps they would, but if so they would only act as the instruments of the gods. The gods had decreed her death to save the world from demons. The demon in the swords grew strong. If he grew much stronger, he might break the shackles that banished his brethren from the world.

Asana rested a hand on her shoulder, and for the first time she saw tears in his eyes.

"Let not your heart be troubled, old friend," she said to him. "Life for me is well lived if only I defeat the shamans, and that might yet come to pass. I need not live beyond that."

Thus ends *Swords of Ravens*. The Shaman's Sword series concludes in book eight, *Swords of Deception*, where Shar stands in the very maelstrom of the battle between the Light and the Dark…

SWORDS OF DECEPTION

BOOK EIGHT OF THE SHAMAN'S SWORD SERIES

COMING SOON!

Amazon lists millions of titles. Don't miss out when I release a new one. Join my Facebook group – *Home of High Fantasy* to keep up to date. There we also discuss all things epic fantasy – books, music and movies. It's a treasure hoard of the things we love!

If Facebook groups aren't your thing, follow me on Amazon. Just go to one of my book pages, click my name near the title and then follow.

Dedication

There's a growing movement in fantasy literature. Its name is noblebright, and it's the opposite of grimdark.

Noblebright celebrates the virtues of heroism. It's an old-fashioned thing, as old as the first story ever told around a smoky campfire beneath ancient stars. It's storytelling that highlights courage and loyalty and hope for the spirit of humanity. It recognizes the dark, the dark in us all, and the dark in the villains of its stories. It recognizes death, and treachery and betrayal. But it dwells on none of these things.

I dedicate this book, such as it is, to that which is noblebright. And I thank the authors before me who held the torch high so that I could see the path: J.R.R. Tolkien, C.S. Lewis, Terry Brooks, Susan Cooper, Roger Taylor and many others. I salute you.

And, for a time, I too shall hold the torch high.

Appendix: Encyclopedic Glossary

Note: The history of the Cheng Empire is obscure, for the shamans hid much of it. Yet the truth was recorded in many places and passed down in family histories, in secret societies and especially among warrior culture. This glossary draws on much of that 'secret' history, and each book in this series is individualized to reflect the personal accounts that have come down through the dark tracts of time to the main actors within each book's pages. Additionally, there is often historical material provided in its entries for people, artifacts and events that are not included in the main text.

Many races dwell in Alithoras. All have their own language, and though sometimes related to one another the changes sparked by migration, isolation and various influences often render these tongues unintelligible to each other.

The ascendancy of Halathrin culture across the land, who are sometimes called elves, combined with their widespread efforts to secure and maintain allies against various evil incursions, has made their language the primary means of communication between diverse peoples. This was especially so during the Shadowed Wars, but has persisted through the centuries afterward.

This glossary contains a range of names and terms. Some are of Halathrin origin, and their meaning is provided.

The Cheng culture is also revered by its people, and many names are given in their tongue. It is important to remember that the empire was vast though, and there is no one Cheng language but rather a multitude of dialects. Perfect consistency of spelling and meaning is therefore not to be looked for.

List of abbreviations:

Cam. Camar

Chg. Cheng

Comb. Combined

Cor. Corrupted form

Hal. Halathrin

Prn. Pronounced

Age of the Archer: One of twelve astrological ages of the Cheng star calendar. All twelve together comprise an astrological year, which constitutes 25,772 regular years. This vast epoch represents the scientific phenomenon known as the precession of the equinoxes.

Ahat: *Chg.* "Hawk in the night." A special kind of assassin. Used by the shamans in particular, but open for hire to anybody who can afford their fee. It is said that the shamans subverted an entire tribe in the distant past, and that every member of the community, from the children to the elderly, train to hone their craft at killing and nothing else. They grow no crops, raise no livestock nor pursue any trade save the bringing of death. The fees of their assignments pay for all their needs. This is legend only, for no such community has ever been found. But the lands of the Cheng are wide and such a community, if it exists, would be hidden and guarded.

Alithoras: *Hal.* "Silver land." The Halathrin name for the continent they settled after leaving their own homeland. Refers to the extensive river and lake systems they found and their wonder at the beauty of the land.

Argash: *Chg.* "The clamor of war." Once a warrior of the Fen Wolf Tribe, and leader of a band of the leng-fah. Now chief of the clan.

Asana: *Chg.* "Gift of light." Rumored to be the greatest swordmaster in the history of the Cheng people. His father was a Duthenor tribesman from outside the bounds of the old Cheng Empire.

Bai-Mai: *Chg.* "Bushy eyebrows." One of the elders of the Nashwan Temple. And the traitor who oversaw its destruction.

Boldgrim: A member of the Nahat.

Chatchek Fortress: *Chg.* "Hollow mountain." An ancient fortress once conquered by Chen Fei. It predates the Cheng Empire however, having been constructed two thousand years prior to that time. It is said it was established to protect a trade route where gold was mined and transported to the surrounding lands.

Chen Fei: *Chg.* "Graceful swan." Swans are considered birds of wisdom and elegance in Cheng culture. It is said that one flew overhead at the time of Chen's birth, and his mother named him for it. He rose from poverty to become emperor of his people, and he was loved by many but despised by some. He was warrior, general, husband, father, poet, philosopher, painter, but most of all he was enemy to the machinations of the shamans who tried to secretly govern all aspects of the people.

Cheng: *Chg.* "Warrior." The overall name of the various related tribes united by Chen Fei. It was a word for warrior in his dialect, later adopted for his growing army and last of all for the people of his nation. His empire disintegrated after his assassination, but much of the culture he fostered endured.

Cheng Empire: A vast array of realms formerly governed by kings and united, briefly, under Chen Fei. One of the largest empires ever to rise in Alithoras.

Chun Wah: *Chg.* "Mountain forest shrouded by mist." A general in the Skultic force. Once a monk of the Nashwan Temple.

Conclave of Shamans: The government of the shamans, consisting of several elders and their chosen assistants.

Dakashul: *Chg.* "Stallion of two colors – a piebald." Chief of the Iron Dog Clan.

Dastrin: *Chg.* "Shadow of the forest." Warrior of the Silent Owl Clan, and cousin to the chief. With Shar's help, elevated to the chieftainship.

Discord: The name of Kubodin's axe. It has two blades. One named Chaos and the other Spite.

Dragon of the Empire: One of the many epithets of Shulu Gan. It signifies she is the guardian of the empire.

Dragon's Breath Inn: An inn in Nagrak City secretly owned by Shulu Gan and a hub for one of her spy networks.

Duthenor: A tribe on the other side of the Eagle Claw Mountains, unrelated to the Cheng. They are breeders of cattle and herders of sheep. Said to be great warriors, and rumor holds that Asana is partly of their blood.

Eagle Claw Mountains: A mountain range toward the south of the Cheng Empire. It is said the people who later became the Cheng lived here first and over centuries moved out to populate the surrounding lands. Others believe that these people were blue-eyed, and intermixed with various other races as they came down off the mountains to trade and make war.

Elù-haraken: *Hal.* "The shadowed wars." Long ago battles in a time that is become myth to the Cheng tribes.

Fen Wolf Tribe: A tribe that live in Tsarin Fen. Once, they and the neighboring Soaring Eagle Tribe were one people and part of a kingdom. It is also told that Chen Fei was born in that realm.

Fields of Rah: Rah signifies "ocean of the sky" in many Cheng dialects. It is a country of vast grasslands but at its center is Nagrak City, which of old was the capital of the empire. It was in this city that the emperor was assassinated.

Fury: A primeval creature of magic. Associated with vengeance and retribution. Animalistic, but can take on human form.

Gan: *Chg.* "They who have attained." It is an honorary title added to a person's name after they have acquired great skill. It can be applied to warriors, shamans, sculptors, weavers or any particular expertise. It is reserved for the greatest of the best.

Green Hornet Clan: A grassland clan immediately to the west of the Wahlum Hills. Their numbers are relatively small, but they are famous for their use of venomed arrows and especially darts.

Halathrin: *Hal.* "People of Halath." A race of elves named after an honored lord who led an exodus of his people to the land of Alithoras in pursuit of justice, having sworn to defeat a great evil. They are human, though of fairer form, greater skill and higher culture. They possess a unity of body, mind and spirit that enables insight and endurance beyond the native races of Alithoras. Said to be immortal, but killed in great numbers during their conflicts in ancient times with the evil they sought to destroy. Those conflicts are collectively known as the Shadowed Wars.

Huigar: *Chg.* "Mist on the mountain peak." A bodyguard to Shar. Daughter of the chief of the Smoking Eyes Clan, and a swordsperson of rare skill.

Iron Dog Clan: A tribe of the Wahlum Hills. So named for their legendary endurance and determination.

Kubodin: *Chg.* Etymology unknown. A wild warrior from the Wahlum Hills, and chief of the Two Ravens Clan. Simple appearing, but far more than he seems. Asana's manservant and friend.

Leaping Deer Tribe: A clan of the Nahlim Forest.

Letharn: *Hal.* "Stone raisers. Builders." A race of people that in antiquity conquered most of Alithoras. Now, only faint traces of their civilization endure.

Magic: Mystic power.

Maklar: *Chg.* "Tall antlers." Chief of the Roaring Stag Tribe.

Malach Gan: *Chg.* "Pearl of many colors, plus the honorary gan – master." A lòhren and a shaman of ancient times. Perhaps still living.

Master Kaan: *Chg.* "Peace of a mountain valley." Abbot of the Nashwan Temple.

Nahring: *Chg.* "White on the lake – mist." Chief of the Smoking Eyes Clan, and father of Huigar. Rumor persists that his family possesses some kind of magic, but if so it has never been publicly revealed.

Nagrak: *Chg.* "Those who follow the herds." A Cheng tribe that dwell on the Fields of Rah. Traditionally they lived a nomadic lifestyle, traveling in the wake of herds of wild cattle that provided all their needs. But an element of their tribe, and some contend this was another tribe in origin that they conquered, are great builders and live in a city.

Nagrak City: A great city at the heart of the Fields of Rah. Once the capital of the Cheng Empire.

Nahat: *Chg.* "A gathering of fifty." A group of shamans splintered away from the shaman order.

Nahlim Forest: *Chg.* "Green mist." An ancient forest in the west of Cheng lands.

Nakatath: *Chg.* "Emperor-to-be." A term coined by Chen Fei and used by him during the period where he sought to bring the Cheng tribes together into one nation. It is said that it deliberately mocked the shamans, for they used the term *Nakolbrin* to signify an apprentice shaman ready to ascend to full authority.

Nashwan Temple: *Chg.* "Place of rocks." A holy temple in the region of Nashwan in the Skultic Mountains.

Nassa: *Chg.* "The snake that hides and waits." A member of the Ahat. In his younger days he led a team of assassins that specialized in the killing of shamans.

Nazram: *Chg.* "The wheat grains that are prized after the chaff is excluded." An elite warrior organization that is in service to the shamans. For the most part, they are selected from those who quest for the twin swords each triseptium, though there are exceptions to this.

Night Walker Clan: A tribe of the Wahlum Hills. The name derives from their totem animal, which is a nocturnal predator of thick forests. It's a type of cat, small but fierce and covered in black fur.

Ngar River: *Chg.* "Deep cleft." A great river that runs north-west from the Skultic Mountains into the sea. In places it runs deep through softer stone forming narrow canyons.

Nogrod: *Chg.* "Aisle of tree trunks." Chief of the Leaping Deer Tribe.

Olekhai: *Chg.* "The falcon that plummets." A famous and often used name in the old world before, and during, the Cheng Empire. Never used since the assassination of the emperor, however. The most prominent bearer of the name during the days of the emperor was the chief of his council of wise men. He was, essentially, prime minister of the emperor's government. But he betrayed his lord and his people. Shulu Gan spared his life, but only so as to punish him with a terrible curse.

Radatan: *Chg.* "The ears that flick – a slang term for deer." A hunter of the Two Ravens Clan.

Ravengrim: One of the elders of the Nahat.

Roaring Stag Tribe: A Cheng tribe located in the Nahlim Forest.

Runeguard: One of the elders of the Nahat.

Rushkatar: Etymology unknown. Chief Elder of Tashkar City.

Shadowed Wars: See Elù-haraken.

Shaman: The religious leaders of the Cheng people. They are sorcerers, and though the empire is fragmented they work as one across the lands to serve their own united purpose. Their spiritual home is Three Moon Mountain. Few save shamans have ever been there.

Shar: *Chg.* "White stone – the peak of a mountain." A young woman of the Fen Wolf Tribe. Claimed by Shulu Gan to be the descendent of Chen Fei.

Shulu Gan: *Chg.* The first element signifies "magpie." A name given to the then leader of the shamans for her hair was black, save for a streak of white that ran through it.

Silent Owl Tribe: A Cheng tribe located in the Nahlim Forest.

Skultic Mountains: Skultic means "the bones that do not speak." It is a reference to the rocky terrain. The mountains rise up in proximity to the Nahlim Forest.

Smoking Eyes Clan: A tribe of the Wahlum Hills. Named for a god, who they take as their totem.

Soaring Eagle Tribe: A tribe that borders the Fen Wolf Clan. At one time, one with them, but now, as is the situation with most tribes, hostilities are common. The eagle is their totem, for the birds are plentiful in the mountain lands to the south and often soar far from their preferred habitat over the tribe's grasslands.

Swimming Osprey Clan: A tribe of the Wahlum Hills. Their totem is the osprey, often seen diving into the ocean to catch fish.

Taga Nashu: *Chg.* "The Grandmother who does not die." One of the many epithets of Shulu Gan, greatest of the shamans but cast from their order.

Tagayah: Origin of name unknown. A creature of magic and chaos, born in the old world long before even the Shadowed Wars, but used during those conflicts by the forces of evil.

Targesha: *Chg.* "Emerald serpent." Chief of the Green Hornet Tribe.

Tashkar: Etymology unknown. A trade city close to the Ngar River. Wealthy, and renowned for its wheat harvests grown on the fertile river flats.

Three Moon Mountain: A mountain in the Eagle Claw range. Famed as the home of the shamans. None know what the three moons reference relates to except, perhaps, the shamans.

Traveling: Magic of the highest order. It enables movement of the physical body from one location to another via entry to the void in one place and exit in a different. Only the greatest magicians are capable of it, but it is almost never used. The risk of death is too high. But use of specially constructed rings of standing stones makes it safer.

Tsarin Fen: *Chg.* Tsarin, which signifies mountain cat, was a general under Chen Fei. It is said he retired to the swamp after the death of his leader. At one time, many regions and villages were named after generals, but the shamans changed the names and did all they could to make people forget the old ones. In their view, all who served the emperor were criminals and their achievements were not to be celebrated. Tsarin Fen is one of the few such names that still survive.

Two Ravens Clan: A tribe of the Wahlum Hills. Their totem is the raven.

Uhrum: *Chg.* "The voice that sings the dawn." Queen of the gods.

Wahlum Hills: *Chg. Comb. Hal.* "Mist-shrouded highlands." Hills to the north-west of the old Cheng empire, and home to Kubodin.

About the author

I'm a man born in the wrong era. My heart yearns for faraway places and even further afield times. Tolkien had me at the beginning of *The Hobbit* when he said, ". . . one morning long ago in the quiet of the world . . ."

Sometimes I imagine myself in a Viking mead-hall. The long winter night presses in, but the shimmering embers of a log in the hearth hold back both cold and dark. The chieftain calls for a story, and I take a sip from my drinking horn and stand up . . .

Or maybe the desert stars shine bright and clear, obscured occasionally by wisps of smoke from burning camel dung. A dry gust of wind marches sand grains across our lonely campsite, and the wayfarers about me stir restlessly. I sip cool water and begin to speak.

I'm a storyteller. A man to paint a picture by the slow music of words. I like to bring faraway places and times to life, to make hearts yearn for something they can never have, unless for a passing moment.

Printed in Great Britain
by Amazon